The Wedding

The Wedding

ISBN 978-1-948613-22-4

Library of Congress Control Number: 2023912331

Printed in the United States of America

Sunny Day Publishing, LLC
Cuyahoga Falls, Ohio 44223
www.sunnydaypublishing.com
editor@sunnydaypublishing.com

Also by Kelly Smith

Out Of The Darkness, June 2021

After enduring an abusive, toxic relationship, what do you do when you leave? You heal. In *Out of the Darkness,* the follow up to Kelly's first book *Signs in the Rearview Mirror, Leaving a Toxic Relationship Behind,* Kelly takes you on her journey of her healing process recovering from her own past abusive tendencies and her previous toxic relationship. Dating soon follows and so do the bad and unhealthy dates. A life-changing trip to Europe with a friend shows Kelly what she's truly looking for in a healthy relationship. With eyes wide open, Kelly meets Cruz. They click right away and as they move forward together, Kelly guides you throughout her firsts in her new healthy relationship after healing from a toxic relationship. What does a healthy relationship look like after abuse? Find out in *Out of the Darkness.*

Signs In The Rearview Mirror: Leaving a Toxic Relationship Behind, April 2018

What kind of person ends up in a toxic relationship? And why does she stay? This searingly honest novel answers both those questions head-on. Coming out of a failing marriage, Kelly turns to Gabe out of fear of being alone. Her gradual slide into danger is at once terrifying and inevitable, and the steps she takes to get out of it will both inspire and offer hope.

They will tell you
you can't do it…
you did.
Keep making the words go,
I am proud of you.

The Wedding

KELLY SMITH

One

Introductions

One by one as people arrived at one of the city's hottest spots for high-end nightlife, they were treated like royalty. The Planetarium, an invitation-only rooftop bar, was a hot spot not only for anyone not attached in a relationship, but for anyone wanting to have fun at Boston's premier summer outdoor nightclub. Because the venue was a desirable place to be, the guests began to flow in like waves on a beach. As they entered The Planetarium, on a warm evening in August, with their rose gold and sparkling invitations in hand, they were led to the glass outdoor elevator where a view of the city was slightly beginning to light up the early August night. This was the first attraction for these "Single in the City" singles, exclusive clientele who were invited to this swanky "White Party, Red Shoes" event as the dating app was branching out into matchmaking.

After exiting the elevator and exchanging their invites for a glass of bubbling champagne, they followed the red carpet to a room full of extensive crystal solar systems highlighting the constellations of Orion, Hydra, and Ophiuchus, that glowed soft hues gradually changing colors. Just outside on the balcony, telescopes were set up to view the stars that were now beginning to surface in the twilight sky all around them. Behind the hustle and bustle of the room beginning to fill, Piper, wearing an off-white mini dress that displayed her long legs but took nothing away from her dirty blonde hair and brown eyes. She stood in the middle of the extravagant venue and made sure everything was in place. As she stood there, swimming in the idea of what tonight could bring, she allowed her mind to wander. She wondered if maybe she would meet someone. Wondered if tonight would be the night. Blake, the ex-boyfriend she left behind in her hometown so she could better her career, crossed her mind. For a split second she wondered if she had made a mistake. Just as she thought about him, the DJ warmed up the night with his first set.

As she continued to scan the room with music in her ears and her mind now focused on the night unfolding before her, she saw women dressed in shiny, tight-fitting white dresses and red high heels. Some wearing dresses with thigh high slits and others twirling to see their knee-length dress move in the self-inflicted wind. The men were handsome, groomed, and the room was a full cologne buffet. Some men were in bright white suits with red loafers and others in tight-fitting tees and white jeans with red Converse sneakers.

Piper moved from the middle of the room to the balcony and made her way to the front door, scanning the room for her friends. Just as she made it to the glass elevator, the door opened and out walked her friends.

First, she spotted Grace. Her red, open-toed strappy high heels walked off the elevator first, and from there, the rest of her followed wearing a tight white, open-chested dress with flowers sporadically placed covering the dress that was clearly made for her. Her long blonde hair was pulled tight into a high pony, her green eyes sparking, and her make-up was flawless. From the way she walked off that elevator you would have no idea that she and her longtime boyfriend, Cory, had broken up mere months ago.

Close behind her was Rachel, the most mysterious friend. Rachel, with her black hair straightened down her back, and her unusual gray eyes, was dressed in an eggshell, strapless, knee-length summer dress. Rachel had moved to Boston a few years ago trying to get over Marcus, a man she dated for years. They could not manage to work things out in their relationship, so they parted ways. Although they all knew she was still in love with him, she would argue to the death that she was still healing and that's why she didn't date very much. She didn't talk much about him, but when she did, her face lit up. The mystery of how it all went down was yet to be talked about.

Sydney, the token red head of the group, slid off the elevator in the shy manor they would all expect. Her floor-length, summer flowing pearl-white dress was something you could tell Grace forced her into. After the death of her almost-fiancé Daniel, Sydney was coming out of her shell, but she felt as if she wasn't quite ready to date all the way because she had a few short-lived relationships that didn't turn out the way she expected but, her friends knew better. They knew the right guy would bring her all the way out of her shell, so they all encouraged her to show up to Piper's event. As Sydney put her hands in the pockets of her borrowed dress, she looked around awkwardly until she was handed a glass of champagne and her hazel eyes met Piper's.

Piper made her way to her friends, and they all joined in on a group hug with a few squeals releasing as they squeezed tight.

"Wow Piper!" Grace said as she made a full 360 turn with drink in hand, "this place looks amazing. You outdid yourself."

"Yeah," Sydney chimed in, "it's beautiful."

Rachel walked to the edge of floor to ceiling window, taking in the view of the city below. "I love this, Piper. Is your boss happy? Has she seen it yet?" Rachel asked as she sipped from her glass, leaving a lipstick imprint along the rim.

"She's not here yet, but she should be soon. I am so happy with the turnout so far," Piper said, eyes searing to the room, now fuller than it was moments ago. "I am so happy she gave me this opportunity to showcase my talents."

"You did give up a lot to be here," Grace said.

"Yeah," Piper said as she looked around the large extravagant venue, she spent months preparing for. She knew it was worth it, but at what cost? In that moment she could not help but think of Blake once again.

It had been two years since she had spoken to or seen Blake. In those two years Piper took her dream job as the head of marketing for TOGETHER, an online dating app. She spent her time meeting new people, planning events, talking to clients, and trying to figure out how to improve the swiping app. Although she was around and could have access to profiles, Piper was just not in a place where she was ready to date. She had left the love of her life to begin something new for herself.

On the day she had made the decision to choose herself over her relationship with Blake, in the back of her mind she figured he would come around to her living in the city and suck it up and move to be with her, but when that didn't happen, Piper's heart hardened and she refused to let anyone in, regardless of who showed up in her life.

Through the grapevine, she heard Blake moved out of Ardentville. She had heard that living in the small town without her was just too painful. He took a job as a photojournalist and began to travel. When she heard this, it surprised her because his passion was cars, not photography. Photography was a hobby for him. She had seen his work and he was amazing, but his face always lit up when he talked about cars, repairing them, and bringing them back to life. His dad owned one of the only car repair shops in town. She thought, before she got her big city job, that they would get married, have a couple kids. He would work at the shop, and she would become a marketing agent in town. But when she got her job offer for TOGETHER, everything changed. She wanted to do all of that but in the city. Blake didn't. He wanted to stay in town and build a life with her there. Piper turned to her mom for advice.

"I don't know what to do," Piper said through tears while sitting in the living room at her mom's house. "I had no idea I would ever get a job offer like this. It is incredible. With the salary, I could live in Boston and still have a life," she said, "but Blake. Oh my God, Mom. Blake. He wants to stay here and build a life here with me. I love him so much, but I am not sure I can give up a job like this to live here. Don't get me wrong, I love it here, but this opportunity is amazing," she cried out as she fell into her mother's lap, covering her face with both hands and sobbing.

"Piper. Look at me," Lucy said as Piper looked up and made eye contact with her mom. "It is going to be okay. You will not make the wrong decision regardless of what you choose to do. You must do what's best for you. You. Not Blake. Not your relationship. You. So, Piper, go wash your face, clear your head, and then decide," Lucy said sternly yet lovingly.

"Piper!" Stephanie, her boss, called out, snapping Piper back to reality. "This place looks incredible," Stephanie said as she intertwined her arm in Piper's arm and they walked off together.

Piper looked back at her friends and mouthed "I'm sorry," and she was gone.

"Well ladies, let's have some fun tonight!" Grace said as she swigged her champagne.

"OK, before we get into the fun section of the night," Rachel said grabbing her friends by their arms, pulling them toward a round-top bar table, "let's get on the same page with what's going on with Cory," she said, taking away Grace's glass.

Grace slumped her shoulders like a small child not getting her way and tried to reach for her glass. When Rachel would not give it back, Grace knew accountability had entered the chat.

"I'm okay. I'm feeling better about it. After moving into my new place, and taking some much-needed time for me, I'm ready to date and see if I can find what I'm looking for," she said.

"Well, what are you looking for?" Rachel asked.

"Someone who is ready and wants to have a family. I want to be a wife. I really do. I don't want just a wedding, I want a husband, you know?" she asked.

"Why didn't it work with Cory again?" Sydney asked, knowing full well Grace jumped the gun by breaking up with him and hoped if she heard herself say it, something would click for her.

"He didn't want to get married," she said matter of factly.

"What did he say? Tell us again how your relationship ended," Rachel asked, following Sydney's lead.

Grace took a minute and wondered why they were asking about this again, maybe she didn't say all of it, maybe she was drinking when she told the story of it, so she wanted to be sure she got all of it out this time, so she started from the last day they spent together, not knowing then that it would be the last day they spent together.

Two

Misunderstandings

As they lay in bed, Grace discovered Cory had no interest in getting married now or, possibly, ever. They never really had the marriage and kids conversation before moving in together. She felt as if they never needed to because it never came up, and assumed they were both on the same page.

"So, what are you saying?" Grace looked at Cory with wide eyes slowly filling with tears.

"I don't know Grace; I am not sure I want to get married. I'm not sure it's something I want, at least not now," he watched as she inched farther away from him. He took a breath and continued, "not for a while anyway. I'm still working on my career, and I'm not sure I can do both."

"But isn't that what happens after you move in with someone? Don't you get married and have kids?" she asked with tears now rolling down her face.

"I have no idea what is supposed to happen. I just know that I like the life we have now. Why does it have to change?" he asked, confused.

"Because. I need to know if you want to get married. I want to get married. I want to have kids and if you don't then what is the point of all of this?" Grace's annoyance was slowly turning into anger.

"I thought the point of all this was to be happy and
see how it goes?" he said, scooting closer to her as she
now sat at the edge of the bed.

"See how it goes?" she yelled as she got off the bed
and turned to face him. "What does that even mean?
So, like, to live together with no end in sight and hope
something more comes from this? What about what I
want? Does that even matter to you?"

"Of course, it matters to me Grace, I love you, but I
can't predict the future. I need to build my career and
get on my feet before I have a wife and then kids. Please
try to understand where I'm coming from," he begged.

"I can't. It makes no sense to me that you can't even
say you want to get married someday. I am not sure I
want to do this with you anymore, Cory. I need stability," she said as she looked down and away from him.

"You can't?" he said, confused. But his confusion
was turning into anger as well. "How can you just give
up like this? Can you try to see this from my point of
view?" his tone turning stern.

He did have a point, and maybe things could have
been worked out if there was understanding on either
side, but as his words fell from his mouth, Grace's visions of wearing a white dress and seeing Cory waiting for her at the end of a long aisle in an enormous
church filled with closest friends and family went up in
smoke. The flashes she saw of him rubbing her pregnant
stomach, opening gifts at their baby shower, and then
walking their children into their first day of school, disappeared into thin air. As she came back to reality, her
face met his and the words he then said shattered her
world.

"I'm guessing your silence answers those questions. I can be gone by tonight if this, us, is something you no longer want," he said directly, coldly.

Her stomach dropped. She felt as though she had been sucker punched and had no words to respond. So, instead, she just nodded. He got up, got dressed and walked out of the room.

"Have you guys talked since? Do you think it's too late? Do you miss him?" Sydney asked in a rapid-fire way, while looking straight at Grace.

Grace looked at her friends, and then away.

"What is it? What did you do?" Sydney questioned, knowing the guilty look on her friend's face.

"I called him," she admitted, "after he moved out and after I made a spectacle of myself," she lowered her head. "I drank too much one night a few weeks later and I called him. I was afraid I made a mistake, and I wanted to see if we could work things out," Grace took a deep breath and Rachel handed her back her drink and looked over at Sydney, and they were both in shock to hear Grace called him.

"What did he say?" Rachel asked.

"He said he felt as if I abandoned him. That he thought about me all the time but was afraid to try again because he wasn't ready to get married and that I could just walk away, and he was not sure if he could handle losing me all over again. He didn't want to promise something he was not sure he could follow through with and he didn't want me to make a sacrifice and later on resent him for it," she paused, took a large gulp of champagne finishing it off. "I lost him. But I'm getting better. I don't think of him as much and I am thinking about dating. Speaking of," Grace said as she pointed her finger around the now-full venue, "I think we need to get talking to a few of these men," Grace grabbed another drink off the server's tray as he walked by.

"You go ahead," Rachel said, "I'm going to go to the ladies' real quick."

"You okay?" asked Sydney. "You want me to go with you?" she asked as she grabbed Rachel's hand.

"I think I'm okay," Rachel said as she squeezed Sydney's hand back. "But, yeah, can you go with me?" she asked with a half-smile and tears building behind her gray eyes.

Sydney linked arms with Rachel and led the way through the crowd of singles and toward the bathroom doors near the elevator. As they made their way to the bathroom, they passed by men and women laughing, drinking, and making small talk. The music that was filling their ears got lower and the crowd noises began to settle as they opened the door to the restroom and Rachel lost it.

She fell into Sydney's arms and sobbed. Sydney held Rachel up and managed to walk her to the lounge just outside of the bathroom stalls. They sat on the couch surrounded by fluffy navy blue and white pillows, floor length mirrors framed with crystals, and white carpeting. As patrons walked in and out, some stopping to ask if Rachel was okay, and others just ignoring the friends, Rachel began to open about her sadness.

"I left him," Rachel cried out.

"What? Left who?" Sydney asked as she attempted to wipe away the mascara running down Rachel's cheeks.

"Marcus," she sobbed, "I left him because he always put work first. He chose work over me. He chose friends over me. At first, we were happy, then he got comfortable and no matter what I said he brushed me off, so I left, and being here tonight, with love in the air," she said sarcastically, "was just too much for me."

"When you say you left, what do you mean? You broke up?" Sydney asked, confused. She knew about Marcus, but Rachel didn't say much about him or why they broke up. She always thought it was a mutual thing, no big deal, up until now.

"No Syd. I left and didn't tell him I was leaving,"

"Oh, wow Rachel. Why would you do something like that?"

Rachel wiped her face, inhaled, and began to tell Sydney about the day she left Marcus.

Marcus had just gotten home from a long day of work, now sitting on the couch in his sweats and T-shirt, with a glass of wine.

"I have exciting news!" Rachel said as she sat excitedly next to him on the couch with her own glass of wine. Marcus taking a sip of wine, and looking at her, she instantly knew what he was going to say. The same thing he always seemed to say when she had something to tell him. The same thing he always said regardless of if she was happy, sad, or mad.

"Can it wait?" he asked in an unintentional bothered tone, "I had a long day and right now I just want to relax. Can we talk later?"

Rachel, fed up, got up off the couch put her glass of wine on the sofa table behind them, grabbed her offer letter and threw it at him. "I got the job," she said angrily, "I got the job I have been working for years to get. They want me to work for them. A publishing house interviewed me, had a conversation with the heads of the company and they picked me. *Me!*" she was now shouting. "I have been trying to talk to you about this. I have been putting off the things I have going on in my life so I can support you and your career. Meanwhile, I am emotionally supporting both of us. You are having your needs met and mine are being neglected," she yelled as tears began to race down her now bright red face. "Marcus, I love you, but I need to love myself more. We have been together for over three years, and I am still waiting. Still waiting for date nights, and for vacations, and for us to move in together. I have had enough," she said as she walked to the kitchen, stood over the sink and poured out her wine. She walked angerly as she gathered her things and headed for the door.

"Rachel. Wait," Marcus said, "I am happy for you, I really am. I am proud of you, and I think you are amazing. But you know how important my job is. You know how hard I need to work as a public defender to get to the top and you know that's my goal. I know it's hard at times, but I love you. I don't want you to leave like this," Marcus said as he reached for her.

"No. No Marcus. I have to go. I have given you years of my life. Now it's my turn," she said as she opened the door to his apartment and walked out.

Days later, with no communication from Marcus, and with every fiber of her being completely depleted, Rachel slammed the trunk of her car shut. She stood in front of her apartment building on a busy street and with the warm air around her, she inhaled, closed her eyes, and got into her car. She turned the key in the ignition, put on her sunglasses and slowly drove away from a life she had expected to have with Marcus. Her stomach feeing heavy and empty, she adjusted the rear-view mirror so she could not see her heartbreak as she drove off to what she hoped would be her new life.

"That's so heavy, Rachel," Sydney said as she continued to hold Rachel's hand. "I am so sorry things ended like that. That was a year ago?"

"Yeah, and I still feel sick over it. I just could not take it anymore. If I stayed and gave him another chance it would have been good for a few days and then it would be about him again. It was a cycle I got used to for years. It was going to be hard to leave or hard to stay. I love him and I know if I told him I was leaving he would have convinced me to stay. His words were so colorful when I was upset with him, but when it came down to actually showing up for me, his words were gray again."

"Have you thought about calling him?" Sydney asked.

"Only a million times a day," Rachel said as she looked off in the distance. "I miss him, but I need to put me first. I love my job, and the friends I have made. My life is amazing. I'm trying to move on from him, but it's hard," Rachel explained.

"I get it Rach, I really do. After Daniel died, I had no idea what I was going to do. It's hard to think of loving someone else again when the love is real," Sydney laid her head on Rachel's shoulder.

"Hey Syd," Rachel said.

"Yeah," Sydney responded with her head still gently placed on Rachel's shoulder.

"Tell me the story of how you and Daniel met."

Sydney smiled at the thought of Daniel.

The Proposal

Wearing a yellow floor length maxi dress, she walked through the heavy brown double doors. Upon opening them her eyes were full of light and sparkle. The barn was decorated with twinkle lights, candles, flowers, and a table set for two in the middle of the large space. A carpet led the way to the table setting and she slowly began to walk and take it all in. A crystal chandelier was hanging low enough to be seen but high enough to not be in the way. She turned and looked at him, confused but with a smile on her face she asked,

"Babe, what is this? What's going on?" She continued to walk forward. She grabbed his hand, he squeezed back three times as he let her lead the way.

Once at the table, he pulled out her chair and she could not believe the barn was full of her favorite flowers, lilies. She inhaled and closed her eyes. He sat in the chair across from her and with a smile on his face, he popped open the champagne that was chilling near the table. He poured her a glass and then one for himself.

"I want to make a toast before dinner is served," he said. She looked him and smiled. She held her glass before taking a sip and her eyes were glued to him.

"Love has many shapes and sounds. Love can be messy, and it can be amazing all in the same day. Love can build you up and tear you down. Love can carry you across oceans and then back again. Love can

move mountains and love can bring you back to life. But the trick to love working in this way is finding the right person to not only love, but to love you back in the same way. From the moment I met you, I knew it was you. I knew you were the one I wanted in my life. We took a path that was unlike any fairy tale. We faced sadness, challenges, and near destruction. But here we are today, together. I couldn't imagine my life without you in it. I could not see myself being happy without you. You make me better. I want your happiness, sadness, mood swings, and hangry episodes for the rest of my life." He stood up and got down on one knee. "Will you make me the happiest man in the world and be my wife?"

"Yes!" she cried without hesitation. She stood up and he grabbed her and spun her around. When she landed, still in his arms, he kissed her and then placed the ring on her finger.

Three

Beach Bonanza

Sydney, who normally ran in the evening, enjoyed her run during in the morning the day she met Daniel. That night, she had to work late at Top Notch Pastry Shop baking for the next day. Sofia, her friend and shop owner, had to set up a cake for a wedding. Sydney told Sofia she would fill in for her and Sydney was looking forward to getting some practice in cake building.

That afternoon instead of going to work, she put on her sneakers, hydrated, and made sure her headphones were charged. As she walked out of the door, she made sure she had her inhaler, and she was off. She had planned to run for about an hour on the beach, which she dreaded but after the wine she had the night before, to help get her through another bad date, she needed a good run and a good sweat.

She got to the beach, stretched for a minute, and began to run. After about 30 minutes, she must have tripped over a rock or a shell or something she didn't see, because the next thing she knew she was on her butt and in some pretty intense pain. While sitting on the beach, she managed to get her sneaker off and take a look at the damage to her ankle. It didn't look good, and she knew she needed to get home to put some ice on it.

Just as she stood up, and began to fall, she felt hands on her back and a deep voice coming from behind her. "Watch out there, are you okay?" As he gently placed her on the sand she turned and got a look at her hero. He was a tall muscular guy, short military-style blond hair and the deepest brown eyes she has ever seen. He had a scar on his left cheek, barely noticeable to others but that she noticed right away because of how hard she was looking at him. His hands were soft, but she could feel slight calluses at the same time. As he squatted down to look at her foot, she noticed his shirtless back and how the muscles looked like peaks and valleys. As she scanned his body, noticing his light tan with sweat beads dripping down, it seemed to distract her from the pain her foot was in. He looked up at her and asked, concerned, "What happened here? Looks like we need to get some ice on this before it starts to swell up even more."

Snapping out of her thoughts of his body, and suddenly feeling a sharp throbbing pain in her ankle, Sydney looked at him and muttered, "back that way." Through her pain she pointed her finger like an idiot.

He smiled and she saw the most beautiful, perfectly straight teeth she had ever seen.

"Okay," he said, "I am off in a few minutes, so I can take you home. Let's get moving." He leaned over and picked her up and put her on the back of an ATV that was close by. On their ride back to her house, through a bit of small talk, of him trying to get her mind off the pain she was in, she discovered he was a fireman and worked Beach Patrol on his off days. He tried to work as early as he could because he liked the quiet of the ocean so early in the morning.

When they got back to Sydney's apartment, only

about ten minutes away, he helped her inside, put her on the couch and got her some ice. He took another look at her ankle, now more swollen and bruised, and said he didn't think it was broken, but she should stay off it for a while. He told her to keep ice on it 20 minutes on 20 minutes off and keep it elevated, Motrin for pain. After she was settled in, he said he needed to get going, but gave her his number "just in case" she needed anything. Before he left, he insisted on her number so he could check up on her later. She gladly obliged. And just as fast as he came into her life, he was gone.

About an hour or so after he left, her ankle began to throb, and the pain was getting worse. She hobbled over to her phone and called Sofia. She told her she couldn't make it in to cover her shift. Sofia understood and suggested she get it looked at. Sydney hung up the phone and got in her car. She drove to the urgent care clinic for an x-ray.

After two hours of waiting for results, her cell phone rang. She didn't recognize the number but took a risk and answered it anyway. To her surprise, it was Daniel calling to check on her. She told him where she was and by the time she knew it, he was beside her. Once the doctor came in and told her it was just a bad sprain, she felt relieved. He handed her a prescription for pain and sent her home. Daniel insisted on driving her to the pharmacy and then home again. Once her prescription was filled and she was home on her couch, she popped two pills and Daniel propped two of Sydney's couch pillows under her foot for elevation and then wrapped an ice pack with a hospital bandage securing it to her swollen ankle. He then took a seat next to her after bringing her a glass of water.

"Is this set up, okay? Are you comfortable?" he asked.

"Thanks, I'm good, aside from the pain, but I think that will begin to go away once the pain pills get into my system," she said as she tried to not to look him in the eyes. She was grateful for his help, but also wondered why he was being so helpful. She met him that morning and suddenly he was showing up for her like a boyfriend would. But in that moment, it felt nice to not be alone.

"Okay good. I am glad to help in any way I can. Do you want me to put the TV on?" he asked as he reached for the remote.

"Yes, I have been watching *Dolls*," she said excitedly.

"Really? Me too. Don't tell my friends," Daniel said excitedly, "It's such a great show. Who is your favorite?"

In unison they said "Beth!!" and then laughed as Daniel handed the remote to Sydney who was now the proud owner of a huge smile on her face. She turned on the TV, found her show list and hit *Dolls*. As the show blared and carried on with each "doll" fighting and arguing and drinking in reality, Daniel noticed Sydney beginning to fall asleep. He gently woke her, gave her her next dose of pills for the pain and helped her to bed. As he covered her sleepy body with her blanket, Sydney reached out her hand and grabbed his.

"Thanks Daniel. I appreciate you so much," and she was out. He made sure she would be okay and then, after locking the bottom lock of her front door, he went home.

The next morning Sydney woke up feeling better, sore, but better. She laid in her bed trying to remember how she got there and then suddenly she remembered vaguely that Daniel had helped her. As she began to get herself up, trying not to use her injured foot, she wondered where Daniel was now. Did he stay over? Would he be cooking in the kitchen or sleeping on her couch? When she turned the corner out of her bedroom, she could see both the kitchen and the couch in the living room were empty. She felt a little disappointed but as she made her way to the kitchen, she spotted a note on the table.

Sydney,
I hope as you read this you are feeling better. Although the circumstances in which we met were less than desirable, I am grateful I met you. I would love to take you out on a date if you're willing to go out with me. I will reach out later today to check in on you.
Daniel

Sydney put the note down and with a smile on her face, she hobbled over to her pills, took one and then made herself breakfast.

Later on, that day, as Sydney sat on her couch with her now less-swollen ankle elevated, she heard a knock at the door. She got up and made her way to it. On the other side of the door stood a very nervous Daniel. In his hand he held a bag of almost thawed out peppermint patties. His favorite candy. He didn't want to show up empty handed, his mom taught him better than that, but he also didn't want to be a cliché and bring flowers, so he brought chocolate, in a more casual way. As the door opened, he saw Sydney's red hair first and the green of her eyes, and his stomach dropped, and his mouth dried up. In that moment, seeing her, after taking care of her the previous night, he was feeling something for her.

"Daniel," Sydney said, surprised. "Hi. Come in," she said as she opened the door wider to let him through and noticing the bag of candy he had in his hands. "Peppermint patties, my favorite, but only when they are frozen," she said, hoping they were for her.

"Frozen? You like them frozen? Me too. That's the only way I'll eat them," he said excitedly and handed her the bag, but then realizing she was using crutches to get around, he put them in the freezer for her.

"Thanks so much for yesterday and last night. You were so sweet, helping so much. I have no idea what I would have done if you were not around. My friends went away for a camping trip. They go every year and I'm not into camping, so I stayed behind and my sister lives in Chicago," she explained as she made her way to the couch.

"I was happy to help. I pick up a few overtime hours patrolling the beach in the mornings a few days a week if the hours are available. I am glad I was there to help you. Any idea what you tripped on?"

As the two made small talk, Sydney got comfortable on the couch, and they made plans for their first date. Beach Bonanza was that weekend and Daniel had tickets to all three days. Beach Bonanza was one weekend a year when musicians held mini concerts on the center stage, surrounded by amusement park rides, fried dough, pizza, and everything in between from turkey legs to sit-down dinners. Sydney was excited because Ducky, an international DJ who was making her first American appearance ever, was performing. She had wanted to go but didn't have anyone to go with.

"Do you think I will be okay with my ankle like this?" She asked Daniel.

"I will carry you on my back if I need to," he said with a smile on his face and Sydney had a feeling he was serious. The two agreed to Saturday afternoon and if things went well, Saturday night to see Ducky.

Saturday morning Sydney was feeling better. She was able to put pressure on both feet. Although she had no idea how walking all day may be for her, she was willing to try. She got dressed in shorts, a white v-neck tee and her Converse sneakers. She threw on some makeup and sunblock. Under her casual, Saturday "go to a music fest" outfit, she had on her red bikini in the event they wanted to jump into the ocean.

Daniel was right on time picking her up. They jumped into his car, and they were off. As they got to the event and parked, they could see it was going to be a hit by the size of the crowds already there. They wasted no time. They hopped out of his car and headed through the temporary gates, passing by the handfuls of police officers hired to help keep the peace. As they passed through, Daniel said hello to a few of the officers he knew.

They stood in line for tickets to ride the rides and to play games. As the afternoon heat crept up on them, and the sun got higher and brighter, the pair rode the roller coaster, hit each other in bumper cars, and enjoyed the snacks the venue had to offer. They laughed and talked. They screamed on the big rides and looked at each other as the merry go round went around. Sydney won a bear for Daniel after he failed to hit all the milk containers down and she took pics of him as he hugged it and then he pulled her in close for their first picture together.

As they walked between the rides, games and food stands and with the smells of the ocean nearby, sunblock, and the fried foods mixed around them, Daniel asked Sydney if her ankle was feeling okay. When she told him it was hurting a bit, he found a table nearby, got them a few beers, and they sat talking until the sun set. With their skin warmed from the sun and the evening setting in, they shared their first kiss. Soon after the lights of the makeshift venue turned on, they heard the announcement introducing Ducky. With a quick jump on Daniel's back, the two were off to enjoy the show.

"I loved that story; Ducky is pretty amazing Syd," Rachel said.

"I agree. Are you ready to get back to this 'Single in the City' party and just have some fun?"

"Yes, let's do it," Rachel stood up, grabbed Sydney's hands and they walked back out to the party.

The Usual

Piper: Ladies, are you all awake/home?
Brunch to dish?
Sydney: Why? Just why? It's so early! But yes!
Grace: I have something to tell, so yes!
Rachel: When and where?
Piper: The Usual 30 minutes??

Piper sat at a table set for 4 at The Usual, a popular brunch spot for both locals and tourists alike. The Usual brought in repeat customers not only for their social media presence, but because the food was made fresh to order. The bottomless mimosas were also a fan favorite, each month bringing in a new flavor. Lavender lemonade, the month of August's flavor, sat in front of Piper as she eagerly waited for her friends to arrive so they could dish about the night before.

As the door opened Piper looked up and one by one her friends made their way to the table. The restaurant full of excitement, with a mix of couples, families, and friends recovering from the night before, seemed to quiet down as the friends sat around the old wooden table with a loose leg on one side.

"Hey ladies!" Piper said, as chipper as can be.

"Hey yourself," Sydney said, annoyed. "Why are you so put together so early?"

"Early? It's 11 am. And my trick to looking this fresh" she motioned her hand around her face "is to not drink at an event I planned," she smirked as the waitress came by an took drink orders.

"Let's dish about last night. Who wants to go first?" Piper asked, sipping on her brunch drink and looking around the table of her exhausted friends.

"I'll go," Grace said with a coy smile making its way across her face.

That got the attention of her friends. All three poked their heads up as the waitress delivered drinks for the table and another for Piper.

"Go on," Sydney said placing a straw in her glass.

"I met someone last night," Grace said and put the glass to her lips.

"Wait what?" Rachel questioned thinking back to her saying she misses Cory and looking at Sydney. "Define...met."

"That guy you were talking to just before I left?" Piper questioned.

"Yeah, Daxton," Grace said, looking at her friends.

"Ok, tell us about this guy," Sydney said.

"Well before meeting Daxton, I met a few others..."

First was Nathan, a 38-year-old bank exec who has never been married but was unsure if that was even an option for him or not. Sandy, a dark-haired man from Australia, and the owner of a wildly successful bar just a few blocks away, who seemed to be a great guy with good intentions but was also newly separated. Grace instinctively felt he was not ready, nor looking for, an eventual relationship, which is what she wanted. As she made uncomfortable small talk with Dylan, a college professor of physics, out of nowhere the drink she was holding in her hand splashed from a bump against her back. She felt a sudden wetness running down her backless white maxi. As she turned to see what was going on behind her, she heard a voice.

"I am so sorry," the deep, raspy voice said as he reached for the closest napkin to dry her back off with.

"It's okay, don't worry about it," she said while her eyes met his, "it's so warm out, it felt good," she laughed as she turned her back on Dylan and was now face to face with a handsome, clumsy, man.

As he offered to wipe her now wet back with a napkin, grabbing her shoulder so he could gently spin her around to wipe his drink off her exposed skin, he introduced himself.

"I'm Daxton. It's nice to meet you, despite the circumstance," he said with a slight uncomfortable laugh.

"I'm Grace and likewise," she said with a seductive smile forming from the corner of her mouth as her spin ended and they were now face to face.

She looked him over, up, and down in a matter of seconds. His bald head was shiny, his blue eyes were crystal, his jawline was chiseled and standing before her his muscular frame informed her that he spent time taking care of himself. She noticed his relaxed yet put together outfit: jeans and button-down light gray shirt, causing him to stand out even more amidst the white and red apparel donned by the crowd. His cologne filled her nostrils and made a permanent memory in her mind.

After a few minutes of small talk and exchanges of coy smiles, the two both grabbed a fresh drink and made their way to the closest table near one of the telescopes. As they chatted and laughed, they looked through the lens to see if they could spot clusters of stars. As the night flowed, so did their connection. Grace began to feel something she had not felt since she and Cory broke up. She was laughing with ease and felt more and more comfortable with Daxton as they spent more time together

By the end of the event, Daxton had taken Grace's phone and put his number in it. Then he called himself, so he had her number. After walking her to the door where Piper was gathering her things to leave, Daxton leaned in, put his hand under Grace's chin, pulled her closer and then kissed her on the mouth. Grace kissed him back willingly.

"Can I call you tomorrow?" Daxton asked, still holding her chin, and standing close to her.

"Of course. I look forward to it," Grace said with a smile on her face and an instant kick of excitement on her mind.

Daxton kissed her once more and hugged her good-bye.

Grace swooned. She felt as if her feet were off the ground and her heart suddenly felt a jolt.

The next morning, as Grace opened her eyes and looked out on a new summer day rising over the city and still on her high from last night's encounter, she heard her phone buzz from the kitchen. She lay in bed for a few more minutes, wiped her eyes and stretched until she thought she may throw her back out before lifting her summer comforter off her body. She made her way to the kitchen to grab her phone, but not before starting the coffee maker. As the morning brew scent filled the air, Grace wandered around her apartment opening blinds and turning on the news. She grabbed her mug, and after pouring in her almond milk and one sugar, settled down on the couch and opened her phone. Her eyes widened as she slightly sat up seeing a text from Daxton. She hadn't expected to see his name on her phone so soon after meeting.

"Good morning, beautiful! I hope you slept well," the text read.

She threw herself back against the plush cushion on her couch, careful not to spill her coffee, and just gleamed. At that moment she felt excitement she had not felt in a very long time.

Piper looked at Grace with pierced eyes for a few moments. She then looked at Sydney and Rachel. Piper spoke.

"I don't know Grace. He wasn't dressed like the other guests. What's his deal?" She questioned.

"What do you mean?" Grace asked, "his deal?"

"Yeah, I don't know, something about him was off," she said.

"Off, like how?" Grace asked, getting annoyed.

"I'm sure it's nothing. I saw you guys together talking, and just noticed he was dressed more casually, that's all. But you seem excited about him," she finished.

"I am. He was so nice and seemed really into me," she said, "I am curious to see how this goes with him."

"What are you looking for exactly?" asked Sydney, "I'm only asking because last night you seemed to still miss Cory."

"I mean, I do miss him, but I need to move on. I don't know if I want a full-on relationship, but I want to see where this can go you know? I want to date again and have fun," she explained.

"Well, if you are happy, we are happy," Rachel said as she raised her glass and the other friends agreed. They clinked their glasses together and ordered food.

After their food arrived and a few more drinks in, Piper talked about the success of the previous night.

"What about you guys? Did you leave early? I didn't see much of you after a few hours. Any interest?" Piper asked towards Sydney and Rachel.

Rachel looked at Sydney and they began to laugh. Grace and Piper were confused and demanded to know what was going on.

"Well," Sydney began, "do you remember boat guy?" She asked.

"Boat guy?" Grace asked. "Why does that sound familiar?"

"He was someone I met as I began dating again." she said and then told the story of boat guy...

Hosting weekly baking classes at the local community center led Sydney to meeting new people and teaching what she loved the most, baking. A few of those meetings led to a few dates. One date led her to a short-term relationship and her first sexual experience with someone other than Daniel. At first it was not comfortable for her but after a few times with Anthony, the man she met while dropping his daughter off at one of the gymnastic classes near her baking class at the community center, she began to enjoy sex again.

Anthony was charming and knew how to use his words. The two met up a few nights after meeting at The Silver Fox, in downtown Boston. They had drinks and danced. They shared a kiss later that night and that lead to more dates which eventually lead to her having sex with Anthony. Sex with Anthony was more hard core than the sex she had ever had before. It was more intense and at times unexpected. Like one night they were out with a few of his friends and their spouses. They had spent the day on the water on Anthony's boat.

That night after they docked the boat and took their sun kissed and exhausted bodies to the restaurant at the marina where Anthony kept his boat. As Sydney got up to use the bathroom, Anthony decided he would go too. Anthony followed Sydney to the bathroom. His intention was to go to the men's room, but instead followed Sydney into the women's room, and one thing lead to another and she let it. After having sex in a public place, she wrapped her arms around him, kissing him and then sent him on his way so she could use the bathroom.

"Oh right, the sex-crazed guy who got you back on the horse, so to speak," the group of friends laughed.

"Yes, him. Well, we saw him last night," Sydney said.

"What?" Piper shouted. "I had no idea he was going to be there."

"Yeah, Piper you don't know everything," Grace said in a snarky tone, and Piper made a face at her.

"So did you guys talk?" Piper asked.

"By the time I saw him, I knew it was time to leave the scene. He looked good, but just not for me," Sydney said.

"Did you leave with her Rachel?" Grace asked looking at Rachel.

"Shortly after. I was just exhausted. But I had so much fun. I talked to a few guys. I met Jared, he's an investment banker. He's cute, I gave him my number. I don't think anything will come of it though," she trailed off. Sydney placed her hand on Rachel's leg for support knowing she was still hurting from leaving Marcus. But Sydney wondered did she love Marcus, or did she just feel guilty? Sydney decided she would talk more about this with Rachel.

"So, it's a new week, what do you guys have going on?" Grace asked.

"Well, I have been thinking about running again," Sydney announced.

"No way!" Piper cheered.

"It's nothing crazy, but there is half marathon coming up in November. It's a race for fallen fireman. I figured this is a cause that can get me back into it," she said.

"He would be proud of you, Syd," Grace said, and the others agreed.

"Thanks. It was hard to run after I lost him. At one point I didn't think anything would get me to hang up my sneakers, but I just didn't have it in me, until now," she said satisfied.

As they said their goodbyes, and paid the bill, the friends made plans for their weekly book club meeting and then went their separate ways.

Match Making

Piper was at work. Just as the clock hit 5, Stephanie asked her for a favor.

"I know it's getting late, but can you do me a solid and head to the hospital? I got a call from a young woman saying her surgeon needed help building his TOGETHER profile. I think he may a good candidate for the new match-making service we are rolling out soon," Stephanie stood with her hands together in the doorway of Piper's office and continued, "I know I should have an intern do it, but this guy seems to need some real help."

Piper gave Stephanie an evil eye and asked, "What's the information?"

Stephanie smiled at her and handed her a business card.

"He's expecting you in about fifteen minutes," she said.

"Why does this feel like a trap?" Piper questioned as she grabbed her light sweater and got to her feet.

"Thanks again," Stephanie said as she walked away.

As Piper got in her car, her phone rang. Across the screen on her dashboard, she saw it was her mom.

"Hey Mom, how's it going?" Piper asked, happy to

hear form her.

"Hi sweetheart. I'm okay, I have this pesky headache but other than that I feel good. Matthew is coming by with my grandson and I got him the cutest little outfit and I can't wait to see him in it," she said.

"Oh, that's great Mom, I can't wait to see the hundreds of pictures you send me of him wearing it," she smiled as she looked in the mirror before she stared the car.

"Anyway, with the summer coming to an end, I wanted to see if you would come home for a few days and maybe go to the lake?" she asked.

"I'm not sure I can do that right now, you know with work being busy, but I can see if I can make it work. What do you think?" She asked, not wanting to disappoint her mom.

"Sounds great sweetheart, that's all I can ask for," she said.

"Okay Mom, well I need to head out to do a favor for Stephanie for work, can I call you later?" she asked.

"Oh, sure call me when you have time. I love you sweetheart,"

"I love you too Mom," Piper responded and disconnected the call.

Piper made her way toward the hospital and wondered why she was asked to do this? Is this a setup? Her thoughts were interrupted by another call.

"Hey Grace. What's up?" Piper asked.

"Hi. Are you busy? Can you meet for a quick drink?"

"I wish. I'm running an errand for Stephanie. She has me going to the hospital to help a potential client with his pics and bio for his profile," she explained.

"Really? Why you?"

"Right? I think it's either a set up or someone who

really wants to be matched up. Anyway, what's up?"

"I wanted to talk to you about Daxton," she said and then paused. She knew Grace wasn't a fan of his, but she had no idea why.

"Ok. What's going on with him?" Piper asked.

"Well, I met up with him and I ran into Cory," she said.

"What?! When? How?" Piper shouted.

"That's why I wanted to meet up with you. Any chance you can meet tonight?" she hoped.

"Ah, yes. For sure. I will call you as soon as I finish up at the hospital," Piper assured her.

"Ok great. I'll see if the others are available," and she disconnected the call.

As Piper pulled into the hospital parking lot, she sent a message to her assistant to send her the guest list from the Single in the City event. Something was off with Daxton, and she was going to figure it out.

Piper made her way through the front doors of the hospital and approached the front desk. She stood in front of an older woman with silver hair and glasses that rested on the bridge of her nose. The woman's blue eyes looked through Piper as she rummaged through her bag looking for the card Stephanie had just given her. When she found it a minute later, and handed it to Janet, the older woman sitting behind the desk, Janet made a call and soon a bubbly surgical assistant wearing scrubs was standing in front of her.

"You must be Piper?" the young woman said as she held out her hand to Piper. "I'm Penelope, Dr Melvin's surgical assistant."

"It's great to meet you," Piper said as she shook Penelope's hand.

"Let's have a seat for a minute before I bring you

back to meet Dr. Melvin," she said as she led Piper to a cluster of chairs in the lobby of the hospital.

As the two sat for a few minutes, Penelope explained to Piper that Dr. Melvin had been single for a while and he was not a fan of dating. She described Dr. Melvin, a neurosurgeon, as kind and patient even when he wasn't around his patients. He has a big heart and was over his last relationship, although Penelope didn't know a lot the details of that relationship. Since the breakup he has not had much of a social life. His lifestyle was that of a single man, working out, working, traveling alone, and his passion was cooking.

As Piper listened to this, she wondered why a man like Dr. Melvin needed assistance finding a good woman? When she asked Penelope, she was met with the response she was afraid of.

"His job is intimidating. It also keeps him busy. There have been times when he was out on a date and was called in. A lot of women want a man ready-made. Not many know how to support a surgeon, also," she paused, "surgeons have a bit of a reputation of sleeping with nurses and having a God complex. What people don't know is nurses love the men in blue. They don't always get along with the doctors in a romantic sense, they can be hard to deal with, but Dr. Melvin isn't like that. He's actually a good guy," she explained.

"Well, he sounds like a great catch. No one is perfect. A lot of people have jobs that pull them away from family at times, so I get it." she said but she realized he may not have an easy time finding a woman who could be patient enough to get to know him to find out he's a good guy. "Is he in the back? Can I meet him now?" Piper asked as he looked at the heavy steel double doors that sat behind Penelope.

"Well," Penelope began, "the thing is, he does not actually know you are here," she admitted.

Piper's heart sank, "What?" she asked in disbelief, "What do you mean he does not know I'm here?"

"I knew if I told him you were coming, he would leave early or just say no, so it was better for me to trick him. I guess trick you both, in a way," she said behind a shy face.

"Okay well," Piper said as she got up, "call me when he knows I am here and when he wants me to be here."

"Penelope," a deep voice called form the double doors, "when you are finished, can you come to my office," he said.

"Sure Dr. Melvin. I'll be right there," she said as she noticed Piper and Dr. Melvin locking eyes.

The Announcement

As the friends gathered at their favorite place for happy hour, they settled in and discussed drinks. Wine. Cocktails. Everyone ended up with their usual drinks for the night. As the drinks were swallowed and the friends talked about their weeks of work, relationship issues, and everything in between, the ring was spotted.

"What is this?" she demanded as she grabbed the hand with the giant rock on it.

With nothing but a smile, she blurted, "I'm engaged!!! He proposed a few days ago!!!"

Instantly the girls jumped up and engaged in a group hug.

"Tell us everything!"

As the story of the proposal came to life, the friends listened intently, and the smiles were large and pure.

"I am so happy for you. After all you guys have been through, I could not be happier that you have made it. You are an engaged woman."

"I agree. I had no idea if you guys would make it, but you both really put the work in and now this."

"I am so happy. I had no idea it was coming, and it was truly beautiful. I can't wait for the wedding, but I want to be his wife more than anything," she said with tears in her eyes.

"So now we get to plan the wedding! Do you have dates in mind? Long engagement? Short? OMG are you pregnant?"

"What? No! We just want to be married. We want to be husband and wife. Mr. and Mrs. Kids will come later, much later," said the bride to be.

"Let the planning begin. Let's raise our glasses to our newly engaged friend. I speak for all of us when I say we wish you happiness, health, and a successful marriage. And we will be there every step of the way to support you both! We love you! Cheers!" they all took a sip of their drinks.

She sat in her chair and saw the pure happiness on the faces of her friends, and she knew she had made all the right decisions in her life that lead her to this exact moment. Her dream job. Amazing friends, and a man who would soon be her husband. Life was good. It was now time to plan the wedding.

The Silver Fox

Thirty minutes later after leaving the hospital and meeting Dr. Melvin, Piper sat next to Grace and Rachel at The Silver Fox. The Silver Fox was in downtown Boston, and a central location for all the friends to meet. Grace sipping on a peach ale and Rachel downing her usual tequila drink, Piper ordered a water.

"So, Piper, was it a trap like you thought?" Grace asked.

"Possibly, but tell us about this meeting you called and where is Sydney?" Piper asked looking around.

"She actually found a running coach, so she is with her trainer a few nights a week," Grace said. "She is all in for the half marathon in November."

"Ok, let's make a plan to support her, anyone know where it is?" Rachel asked.

"I think here in the city," Grace said.

"I am so happy for her, but let's get to it. Spill, Grace," Piper said, downing her water.

"I saw Daxton last weekend," Grace said with a smile on her face.

"How did it go? What did you guys do?" Rachel asked.

"And how did you run into Cory?" Grace added.

"Cory? Okay spill it," Rachel said, intrigued.

Grace began to tell her friends about the morning text she received while at home on her couch that led to her, in her mind, exciting day.

"Dax and I were texting, nothing crazy just small talk," she continued...

A few minutes later her phone buzzed; it was Daxton asking if she wanted to meet for coffee. Grace agreed and 30 minutes later and three dress changes before choosing a light pink flowy sundress with light tan wedges, they were standing face to face ordering coffee and muffins at a local cafe.

"So, tell me, how did you end up at last night's event?" Grace asked Daxton as she grabbed her coffee off the counter.

"Ah well, my cousin was the caterer, and he needed some help unloading before the event started. Since I had a free weekend and I have been wanting to check out The Planetarium for a while now, I figured why not?" Daxton smiled and directed her to a table in the back courtyard.

"I had been wanting to check that place out as well. My friend Piper is the marketing director for TOGETHER so that's how I ended up there. But I had no intention of meeting anyone." Grace said with a grin. Daxton smiled back as he pulled out a chair for Grace.

After settling in outside on a quiet Sunday morning under the bright light of the sun, and after a bit of small talk, Daxton looked across the table at Grace and marveled at her. He took in her dark blonde hair and green eyes that shone like emeralds in the daylight. He noticed the glow of her barely there tan complemented the sundress she was wearing. In that moment Daxton felt as if he did not want to lose her. And as she spoke and laughed, her smile took him to places he had never been before.

Entranced, he asked, "tell me everything. Tell me everything about you from top to bottom and leave nothing out." He slid his hand across the table, grabbing hers and squeezing tight. Their eyes met and he saw color rush to her face.

Hours and two more cups of coffee later, Grace had told Daxton everything about her: from being an only child, to winning class president in the sixth grade, all the way through to her breakup with Cory months and months before. As they were throwing away their cups in the nearest bin on their way out, Grace heard a familiar voice say her name.

"Grace?"

It came from behind her. Turning around she was suddenly face to face with Cory.

"Cory?" She was both shocked and slightly excited at the same time.

"Hey, wow. It's good to see you. How, how have you been?" he asked as he motioned to hug her.

Just then Daxton grabbed Grace around the waist and pulled her closer into him, blocking Cory from executing the hug that was headed straight for her.

"Hey, I'm Daxton, and we were just leaving," Daxton said with a stern look at Cory as he grabbed Grace tight by the arm and began to lead her out of the cafe courtyard.

Grace, slightly confused, let Daxton lead her out as she glanced back at Cory with both the look of confusion and distress on her face. Cory, concerned, followed them and called out for Grace. But Daxton held his grip and Grace felt too anxious to look back once more. Cory, thinking Grace wanted to go with Dax-

ton and not realizing she was being forced to go with
him, stopped chasing her when they got close to a car.
When they were on the street, Daxton let go of her arm
and apologized for what had just happened. He said
he thought she looked uncomfortable seeing Cory and
wanted to get her out of there as soon as possible. Grace
looked at her arm, now red, and told Daxton she had
fun, but she had to go.

"Wait!" Daxton called as Grace turned and began
walking to her car. "I am really sorry if I was too aggressive. I was just looking out for your best interest, and I
may have overstepped. Can you forgive me?" he asked
with his blue eyes now looking down as if he were truly
ashamed.

Grace stopped and turned to look at him. Rubbing
her own arm, she thought she saw remorse and could
understand why he did what he did. She began to think
of what he did as sort of sweet. "That was uncalled
for, and I can take care of myself. Please never do that
again," she explained as she walked closer to him.

"Deal," he said with a sad look on his face, and he
opened his arms inviting her in, and she hugged him
tight.

As they reached Grace's car parked a few spots up
from his, Daxton reached over to open the door for
Grace. His arm lightly grazed her breast while reaching past her, which caught her attention. She looked
up at him and made eye contact. Without saying a
word, he motioned for her chin, slid his hand under
it and pulled her face close to his. Without hesitating,
she fell into him and kissed him. Soft at first, but then
more vigorously. She turned to him and moved her hips
closer to his. Slightly moaning Grace was now lost in
him, physically. It had been months since her last sex-

ual encounter with her neighbor downstairs, who recently moved, and she was ready. Her soft moans, as his tongue made itself comfortable in her mouth, made his body react and his hands found their way to the bottom of her sundress. As his hands inched their way up Grace's bare legs and toward her underwear, Grace pulled back, grabbed his hands from under her dress and with heavy breathing coming from her warmed body, she managed to murmur "let's go to my place, it's close." Daxton grabbed her keys, got in the driver's seat, and as Grace gave directions, they impatiently headed to her apartment.

Bursting through the door of Grace's apartment, Grace tossed her keys and bag on the counter and Daxton grabbed her by the waist from behind, kissed her neck and let Grace lead them to the bedroom. As soon as Daxton found the bed, he spun Grace towards him and threw her down, then took off his shirt as he straddled her. Grace, looking up, liked what she saw. She instantly put her hands on his shoulders, with her eyes wide open, she gently traced the outline of them, moving her hands to the back of his triceps and around his biceps. She closed her eyes as her hands blindly moved from his forearms to his chest and eventually around to his back where she grabbed on and pulled him closer into her.

His mouth, now open, sucked on her neck as his hands began taking off her dress. Grace slowly spread her legs wide, and he was eager to fulfill the invitation he was receiving from her.

Hours later, Grace and Daxton sat on her couch in her living room with her legs lying lazily across Daxton's lap. Grace was wearing Daxton's shirt she collected from the floor to replace the bedsheet she was using to cover up. She felt completely content as she gobbled up the Chinese food Daxton ordered for them. As they sat in a bit of silence in her apartment with the sun setting over a calm city summer evening, Grace was snapped out of her happiness when Daxton's phone went off.

"Oh fuck," Daxton said in a low but shocked voice. He pushed Grace's legs off him as he got to his feet.

"What's wrong?" Grace asked.

"I have to go, Grace. Sorry. Something has come up," he said while searching around her apartment to gather his things.

Looking at Grace he asked for his shirt back. Grace took the shirt off, feeling exposed and slightly embarrassed that she was completely naked while he rushed around. And just like that, without so much as a goodbye, Daxton was gone. Grace sat in shock, naked on her couch, wondering what the hell just happened. Minutes later it hit her; they had driven her car to the apartment, his was still at the cafe.

"You slept with him Grace? Just after seeing Cory?" Piper asked reaching for her arm and seeing a bruise. "Grace, you have a bruise on your arm!"

"Do not read into this Piper. It was innocent and was protecting me," she insisted.

"From Cory?! The man you loved and lived with for years?" Piper argued.

"I knew it. I knew you would do this. You know what Piper; I had a great date and I really like him. And he's good in bed!" she shouted across the table.

"Oh, that's great Grace. You have a bruise on your arm but hey the dick was good," Piper snarled back.

"Okay guys, okay let's settle down for a few minutes," Rachel insisted. "Grace, you can see why we have some concerns, right?" Rachel asked.

"I mean I guess, but what am I supposed to do, just stay single forever?" she asked.

"It's not that you are dating again, it's the bruise on your arm," Piper said directly to Grace. "We want you happy with or without Cory, but we don't want you hurt," she continued.

"Yeah, I get it. I can see how it looks, but really it wasn't like that. He was just stepping in where he probably should not have. I'll talk to him," Grace said calmly.

Piper reached for Grace's hand and squeezed it.

"Now it's your turn Piper, tell us about your mystery errand at the hospital," Grace said.

Seven

Moving In

Days after sitting at the happy hour table with Grace and Rachel and telling them about meeting Dr. Melvin, Piper got ready for their first date.

"Hey Syd," Piper said, answering the phone as she gathered her things.

"Hi, so I heard you have a date today? Have a few minutes to fill me in?" she asked.

"Of course, but how is your training going?" Piper asked.

"Oh, it's been so good. My body is sore, but in a good way. I am glad I made this decision. The shop has been going well too. I have been busy getting it ready," Sydney explained. "I have been pulling double duty because I have been short a pastry chef. But I'll figure it out," she finished.

"You still have not been able to find one? Wow, but I am sure you will, I hope soon for your benefit," Piper said as she reached for her lip gloss.

"Okay so spill. Who is this guy? The girls said you seemed excited but were trying to hide it," Sydney asked excitedly.

"Well," she began with a smile on her face, "his name is Rand Melvin. He's a doctor, an actual brain surgeon. Stephanie asked me to go by the hospital to help him with his dating profile. But as it turns out he had no idea I would even be there. His surgical assistant set it up so he could meet someone. Honestly when he found out it was awkward, but Syd, this man is not only handsome, but his personality is amazing, and we seemed to click. I am really looking forward to seeing him today, in a few minutes actually," she said as she noticed the time. "I have to get going, but I am excited you are running again, and if you need my help at the bakery, let me know!" she said, rushed.

"I'll pass on the help, but thank you," Sydney said laughing. "Have fun! Let me know how it goes!" and she disconnected the call.

Sydney placed her phone on the table in front of her. She sat back in her chair in her small apartment and exhaled. She thought about the bakery and tried to figure out how she could hire decent help. She grabbed the ice pack that was lying next to her and wrapped it around her knee. All this running was taking a toll on her body, but she would not have it any other way right now. She leaned all the back and in the still of the silence, she thought back to moving to Boston.

As she stood in front of one of the tallest buildings she has ever seen, she could feel butterflies in her stomach. She knew what she was doing there, in the doorway of her new life, but for the life of her she could not figure out how she got there. She scanned the building and realized it looked different from the website she found it on. It was much older; the red bricks that in the photos were shiny, new, and bright, now looked as if they had either fallen off or were hanging on for dear life, the bright red she expected to see was now a darker flushed out red. She could see the years splashed across the entire building, including the brass numbers that were supposed to be alerting the rushing crowds of where they were, were not as shiny and as she stood there, one of them broke and it started to swing back and forth upside down. The dead plants on the front porch were either a sign of neglect or that winter was fast approaching, either way, it was an eyesore.

As she inhaled deeply and looked around, taking in the neighborhood, she could feel the cold air brush against her face and roll off her cheeks. The sun was out but not for much longer, in the sky she could see shades of blue peeking through the fading cotton white clouds, and the smell of fall was so thick in the air she could practically smell the leaves as they lost their brilliant yellows, reds, and oranges and turned to a crisp brown.

In the distance she could hear sirens. She knew right away they were the screaming sounds of fire trucks. You don't spend as much time as she has around a firehouse and not know the difference between a fire engine, police car, and an ambulance. At the same time, she heard two more roaring engines as they screamed out that someone was in need of help. In front of the fire trucks, she could hear the hustle and bustle of city living, the faint chatting going on between friends, co-workers and probably lovers. The sounds of honking horns, street vendors and whistles calling for cabs all mashed together to create a low roar. She thought she would be able to get used to the roar, but she had no idea she was close to so many fire stations. Thinking about the fire stations made her sick, weak in the stomach.

With the new feeling of butterflies drowning in her stomach, she groped around in her handbag searching for her keys, she climbed the cracked steps that lead to her new life. As she turned the key, she inhaled deeply with her eyes closed, and went inside.

With a smile on her face thinking about a time in her life where she struggled with so much pain and change, she knew what she was facing would not be that difficult. With the ice beginning to melt and her knee feeling somewhat numb, Sydney got up to get ready to head to The Lemon Bar, the bakery she opened when she first moved to the city.

Sydney had a passion for baking. A passion she got from her grandmother. She has no memories before the memories she has baking with her grandmother. Christmas was always the most memorable. Weeks before Christmas Eve, Sydney and her nana would begin to prepare to make the Christmas cookies that the rest of the family and few close friends demanded to have during the family's Christmas Eve party.

Sydney would go to her grandmother's house and at first to study how she made the dough. As the years passed, Sydney was able to make the dough herself. As her grandmother grew older and her hands didn't work as well, Sydney took over the preparations and eventually the decorating as well. Sydney took her passion even further by going to culinary school and was named the best baker of her graduating class, which led to her first job in an upscale restaurant in the small town she lived in.

After Daniel died, she was lost. She left her job, stopped running, and felt as if she was just a shell of a human. It was her grandmother who brought out of her depression by suggesting she move to the city and begin again. As Sydney considered her grandmother's idea, her grandmother passed away. Even more destroyed by two great losses, Sydney's family was worried about her.

Weeks after her grandmother passed, Sydney dis-

covered her grandmother left her money and, in the
will, she specified that the money can only be used to
open a bakery. Along with the check was a letter.

Dear Sydney,

*If you have this letter, it's because I am no longer with
you. I am leaving you this money because I know you are
an incredible baker, and the world deserves to enjoy your
sweet treats and the love you put in them. You losing Daniel was hard and now with the loss of me I know you are
hurting, but I want you to live again. I want you to enjoy
life even again and eventually love again. It's time to get
back to your passion. You know exactly what to do and I
am helping you to achieve your goals. Get ready, get set,
your life is about to begin again. I love you Sydney, make
me proud.*

Love, Nana

Stunned but also with tears running down her face,
she relaxed. Her grandmother was taking care of her
even after her death. Sydney felt inspired and didn't
want to let her nana down. She knew if her nana were
alive, she would be so proud to see how far she has
come. Her grandmother loved lemon bars so when it
came to naming the bakery, Sydney knew without a
doubt what the name would be.

Sydney got up, put the ice pack back in the freezer
and headed toward the bakery. Walking through the
doors of The Lemon Bar, Sydney placed her handbag
on the shelf and began to create. Sydney loved her time
in the bakery when she was alone. She loved to challenge herself and she loved to figure things out on her
own. As she got out ingredients, bowls and turned on
her mixer, her phone buzzed. It was an email with an
invitation to the bakers' seminar in a few weeks.

Eight

Corn Mazes and Candy Apples

Piper sat in the passenger seat of Rand's luxury car while they drove to NewPage toward the fall fest. When Rand called to invite her the fest, she remembered how odd he was on the phone.

"Piper. I am calling because I wanted to discuss the details of our date. I am excited you have agreed to go out with me," Rand said in a stern doctor's voice. Piper felt, for a second, she was a patient awaiting news from a test.

"Well, I am happy you asked," she responded, mocking him in a way. Something he didn't pick up on.

"How is tomorrow late afternoon?" he asked. "I was thinking we could drive to NewPage, to attend their annual Fall Fruit Fest. I hear it is amazing," he continued. "We could leave, say around 3 be there by 4:15 and if we are feeling fallish, we can give their corn maze a shot. I hear it is in the shape of a snowman, because of the heavy winter we are expecting." he said and could not believe he said fallish. His face felt warm and red waiting for her response.

"Rand. Nothing sounds better than feeling fallish. I would love to go with you," she said with excitement in her voice. On the other end of the phone Rand breathed a sigh of relief.

"Great. I will come by and pick you up at three to-morrow," he said, and she agreed.

Sitting next to him now, he seemed more relaxed and less of a surgeon calling to deliver bad news. As Piper sat next to Rand she took in his face, his body, and the way he smelled. His face, she noticed, was sharper than the day she met him in the hospital. That day she was caught off guard and wasn't expecting to meet him in the way she did, a romantic sort of way, a click. She remembered the moment she laid eyes on him that he was attractive, but today sitting close to him in his car, she realized he was absolutely beautiful. Her eyes made their way from his dark skin on his face, to his deep brown eyes and how perfectly his beard was trimmed outlining his perfectly chiseled jaw. Making her way to his chest she noticed how tight his shirt was sitting just beneath the oatmeal-colored cardigan sweater he was wearing. His hands that have opened the skulls of patients, were hugging the steering wheel and Piper suddenly felt warm inside. His legs, although covered in jeans, were sculpted and she knew he didn't miss a day in the gym. Her attention was taken off Rand's appearance when his voice interrupted her thoughts.

"I have been wanting to go to this festival for a while. I am so happy you could go with me. I know it's a long ride, but I think we can make it fun," he said as he looked at her with a bright wide smile and Piper melted a bit noticing how perfectly white and straight his teeth were.

"Yeah, I am excited too," Piper responded realizing her mouth was suddenly dry.

As the two drove to the fall festival, they talked and laughed. They got to know each other as much as they could in a less than two-hour car ride. Rand spoke of his family, his one sister and how his dad was also a neurosurgeon and his mom who was a general surgeon who had a passion for helping others in the ER. He too graduated from Columbia like his parents before him. He talked about his last relationship and how his schedule was too much for Cynthia, and how devastated he was when it ended. As the drive progressed, Piper sat back and listened to Rand tell stories of growing up in Texas, Ethan his best friend who was killed in combat while on tour in Afghanistan, and how his sister married the DA in the city he is originally from. As they got closer to the festival, he explained how he works sometimes at the hospital in Ardentville. Piper mentioned she was originally from Ardentville.

"What? Really? Small world I guess," he said.

"That's crazy and so random," Piper said.

"Yeah, when my colleague Mark asked me to assist him a few years ago, I liked it. I have a small house there actually," he said as he shifted in his seat.

"My mom still lives there; I go visit when I can," Piper said as they pulled into the parking lot of the festival.

The two made their way up Grand Hill. As they walked up the hill, kids and dogs ran past. New parents eager to begin family traditions pushed babies in carriages. Young budding couples held hands and took selfies. Many stayed on the dirt path made by so many people before them, while others ran up and down the hill. Some looked exhausted from the day's festivities holding balloons and bags of fall treats, while others remained excited as they made their way home.

As the sky above them began to turn a darker gray and the chill was suddenly felt by all, Rand grabbed

Piper by the hand and pulled her in a bit closer to let a group of teens pass by. Piper, close to him and inhaling his cologne, let him hold her close. As they arrived at the top of the hill, the view below them was amazing. Looking over the acres of pumpkin patches and apple trees, the lights of the festival kicked on and illuminated the entire festival. In the distance they could hear kids laughing and hushed murmurs of others chatting. Music from the live band began to play and the sun, not quite setting but not quite up, welcomed them to the fall festival. Piper looked at Rand and she saw the smile on his face and for a second, she tried to imagine him as a young child, and she wanted to know what used to make him happy. In that moment she wanted to know everything about him. Rand caught Piper's eye, smiled big at her and the two walked down to the festival hand in hand.

After the sun had set and the chilly air was turning cold, and after they had tasted Mrs. Cooper's famous homemade apple pie, stuffed a scarecrow, taken pictures while lost in the corn maze and dipped apples in caramel, Piper sat close to Rand as they held mugs of hot apple cider in front of the individual fire pits placed by each picnic table. With elbows touching and feelings of happiness swirling above them, they enjoyed a few minutes of comfortable silence.

With the fire close by and the music in the distance behind them, Piper rested her head on Rand's shoulder, seconds later, he placed his head against hers. "I had so much fun with you today, Rand," Piper admitted. "It was exactly what I needed but had no idea I needed. Tonight, right now, feels so peaceful," she said as she closed her eyes, taking in the moment and placing it in the hard drive of her memory.

Over the next few weeks or so Piper and Rand talked, texted, tried to make plans to meet up. But either Rand was called in or Piper had a business trip. The two were independent and career oriented and Piper wondered if anything could come of this.

The Engagement Party

She looked him as they sat in the master bedroom of the house they rented, sitting on the edge of the bed in front of the floor-to-ceiling windows exposing a full view of the ocean. They sat close together, both dressed in white and looking at their family and friends below them laughing, drinking, talking, and celebrating even before the happy couple made their grand appearance. The clambake outside the fence of the backyard was being set up on the beach. Tables and chairs were being placed and the DJ was spinning music at a low volume, but not for long. Hors d'oeuvres were being passed around and from the window they could see their engagement cake next to the gift table.

She grabbed his hand and squeezed three times and he looked at her.

"I love you; you know that, right? Not because I have to say it or because it's expected, I love you because you are incredible. A brat at times and moody, but you have been the best thing to ever come into my life. You made me choose to be a better man," he said now turning to look back outside at the sun just beginning to set.

"And these people," he said pointing his finger in a circular motion, "they are happy for us. They were so supportive of us, and I can't believe after this party, we get to plan our wedding," Now looking at her with tears in his eyes, he said, "and I get to be your husband. It's you and me against the world and I would

not change one moment of our sometimes messed up journey, for anything."

She wiped his tears away from his eyes and gently laid her head on his muscular shoulder, and said, "I simply love all of you, and soon, I get to be your wife. It was a long journey, but I have my person and I am so grateful it's you."

They waited a few more minutes and enjoyed the calm before the party storm and then they got up and made their way to their family and friends.

Nine

Let's Get Honest

The friends were sitting in Rachel's new apartment in the heart of the city for a book club meeting turned new-home viewing. The book club meet-ups were Sydney's idea. She wanted to have get-togethers that were more than just happy hours and dinners. Little did she know how much alcohol would be involved with reading books. Whether someone was celebrating, like Rachel was, falling apart, or just in need of a vent or gossip session, the friends used the book club time to do so. It was something they never missed unless absolutely necessary, and if someone was away out of town, they would skype if they were able to do so.

With Rachel working for a publishing company, it made it easy for her to know which books were coming out and at times she was able to get pre-order books before they hit the bookstores, which would have been a bonus if the friends read the books Rachel brought for them.

"I love this place Rach. I can't believe you were able to get it. It's so beautiful," Grace said, looking out of the window over the city view, "how did you find this place?"

"When I moved here, the publishing company gave

me a 12-month lease a few floors down. When this place became available, I jumped on it. I'm just about done unpacking," she said as she grabbed glasses from a tall shelf near the sink.

"I have the champagne," Grace said, pulling two bottles out of her bag.

"Damn Grace, are we making bad decisions tonight or what?" Piper asked laughing.

"Ha-ha Piper," Grace responded as she opened the first bottle.

Grace poured four glasses of bubbles and they toasted Rachel's new place.

"I never really asked, but how did you find yourself here in the city? Did you look for a job here?" Grace asked.

"Actually, I had another job in California I was on my way to when the publisher called me herself and offered me a job. I got a call…"

"Hello, this is Rachel," she answered the unknown number.

"Hello Rachel, this is Lydia Peterson, from Cuppa Coffee Publishing. How are you today?" Lydia asked in a friendly voice. Rachel, not expecting a call from Cuppa Coffee, was confused yet intrigued as to why she was calling.

"Hi Lydia, I am doing well. How, how are you?" Rachel stumbled over her words.

"Rachel I am calling today, in regard to an article you wrote, "How to Plants Seeds of Love." I have to say that although I don't necessarily agree with the entire article, I love your words and how you write. I looked you up and saw that you are also an editor. In researching you more, I heard through the grapevine that you were just hired at First Amendment Publishing, and I would like to offer you a job at Cuppa Coffee. I would beat the current financial offer they gave you and would like for you to start ASAP. The company has an apartment here in Boston that we would lease to you for 12 months. What do you say Rachel? I know this is short notice, but this offer expires in 24 hours." Lydia said matter of factly.

"So, I literally turned my car around, and here I am."

"California, wow. Your life would have been so different. What did Marcus think of California?" Piper asked sipping her champagne.

Sydney looked at Rachel with big eyes and Rachel looked back at here.

"What? What am I missing?" Piper asked as she slid to the edge of her seat on the sectional couch facing the picture window in the living room.

"You mean what are we missing?" Grace added.

Rachel knew it was time to come clean about Marcus. It had been a year now and it was the right time to begin to let it go so she could begin to move on.

Rachel sat up, placed her glass on the coffee table in front of her. She cleared her throat and her friends followed her with their eyes. The room fell quiet and Rachel spoke.

"I have not talked much about Marcus for a reason. It wasn't just a breakup; it was more than that. But before I go into the details, you should know how much I loved him," she said nervously. She began to tell the story of Marcus.

Years ago, as Rachel got ready for a friend's "Dress

for your Favorite Holiday" themed birthday party, she was running late from work and didn't plan on anything to wear. She ran through her closet to see what she could find. Pulling out her ugly Christmas sweater, she felt as if she struck gold. Pulling it on, she rushed around, trying to freshen up.

"It's no wonder you have not met anyone yet," she said to herself as she looked over her costume for such a stupid birthday theme idea. Making sure the sweater was straight and her makeup was done, Rachel grabbed her keys and headed toward Sal's Place, a dive bar not too far from her apartment. As she parked and walked in not knowing what to expect, she grabbed a drink and chatted with a few friends. Around the room she took notice of the costumes people were wearing in mid-July. A giant man cupid, Santa, elves, a skeleton couple dancing on the dance floor, and one giant blow up turkey. Rachel stood with a group of people feeling as if her "costume" was not costume enough. Feeling a bit awkward and oddly out of place, Rachel planned to go to the bathroom and think of an excuse to leave early. Just as she was turning around to make her way to the bathroom, she bumped into and spilled her drink all over a tall, dark, and handsome man, who unbelievably was wearing the exact same sweater.

"Oh my God. I am so sorry," she said as she placed her now-empty glass on the nearest table and began to search for napkins to help wipe up the mess she made all over his sweater.

"It's okay, it really is," the stranger said as he laughed, Rachel found napkins and quickly began to pat his chest with them. Looking up she saw a bright smile with friendly welcoming eyes looking down at her.

"Really," he said laughing harder now, "it's really okay," he grabbed the napkins from her hands and threw them away. "But we need to find out why we are wearing the same ugly sweater," he said as Rachel looked down at her sweater and then up at his again. "Can I buy you a drink and talk about this sweater thing?" he asked, leading her to the bar with a giant smile on his face.

Behind the sounds of the birthday celebration going on around them at Sal's, the singing, cutting of cake, laughter, and conversations of friends making memories, Rachel and Marcus sat close to each other in matching sweaters and sipped drinks in a corner booth. As they talked about their sweaters, they discovered they bought them at the same place a few years ago and neither one of them had time to put a real costume together for their mutual friend's birthday party so the sweater was logical wear that night. Rachel learned that Marcus was the oldest of four boys. All he ever knew was that he wanted to be a lawyer, and he recently moved to Lakeshore for his job. As time passed Marcus talked about his ex, Sloane. They had been together for a year and half, but things just didn't seem to work out between them. Sloane, although pretty, was "empty minded," he told Rachel.

"We had fun. She was fun. But when it came to real life, the meat of life, she was basic," he said as he looked at Rachel, hoping she would not judge him for being sort of mean about it. "She could handle herself, but she was also selfish. I guess you could say I outgrew her," he continued as he took another sip of his mixed drink. "I realized I was looking for more. More of the good stuff," he said as he clenched his fist tight with passion. "I want to laugh and have meaningful conversations. I want to relax knowing someone has my back if I get sick. If my pieces broke because of a tragedy, I want to know I have someone who is capable and willing to pick up my pieces, if necessary, not kick them around after they shatter. I felt, towards the end, that Sloane would have walked through my pieces while asking me to make her a sandwich at the same time. Sloane was shallow, not capable, or even willing to be that sort of person. There is nothing wrong with that or with her, she just wasn't for me, she was not what I needed her to be in my life," he said as he looked off in the distance. "I knew she was not for me the day she made plans with her friends to tour wineries. Which from the outside looking in is not a big deal right?" He shifted in his seat to get a good look at Rachel's face when he revealed why it was a big deal.

Rachel, intently looking at Marcus, was on the edge of her seat waiting for the rest of the story and sipped her drink as she patiently waited for him to continue. "It was my birthday," Marcus stated matter of factly. Rachel's eyes grew wide, and the swig of alcohol filled her mouth and made her cheeks puff out. As she swallowed hard, she put her hand on Marcus's knee. "Yeah, so that was when I knew it was over. She went. She had fun. And when she got back, I waited. I waited for her to bring a cake or a card or heck, even a bottle of wine. But her friends dropped her off drunk. She slithered into the house, made her way towards me and threw up on the couch. I helped her to bed, but that was it for me. The next day we had a conversation and I left. I moved out. I never want to hurt like that again," Marcus trailed off as the bartender let them know it was ten minutes past closing time.

The two got up and as they looked around, they noticed how empty the bar was. "Wow. I had no idea this place cleared out," Rachel said as she looked for extra cake. As she began to walk, she tripped over nothing. With the bartender noticing the condition they were in, he called them an Uber. They stood in the walkway of the bar entrance, hiding from the sudden summer rainstorm. Marcus asked if he could call Rachel and they swapped numbers. As two Ubers pulled up at nearly the same time, Marcus walked Rachel to the car. He opened the door, and just as she was about to slide in, Marcus grabbed her arm, pulled her close and kissed her on the mouth, and Rachel let him.

Over the next few days Marcus and Rachel texted and had a few phone calls. They used their time to get to know the details of each other's lives. Where they stood with religion, politics, and everything in between. Getting into deep conversations about all of it showed Marcus the depth of Rachel. He enjoyed her thoughts and points of view. Although they didn't always agree on perspectives, they each learned from the other, and both of them loved that. With the weekend fast approaching Rachel took it to the next level by inviting Marcus to Jackson Park Annual Picnic Festival.

Each year Jackson Park hosts a picnic festival to raise awareness of the local cafés and diners. Each setting is set up for lunch and dessert and each café or diner hosts a "picnic placing" to include their best sellers and one meal option. Rachel received two tickets a few weeks prior and was going to give them away, but instead she thought this would be a fun date to go on with Marcus. Marcus accepted her invitation and by Saturday mid-morning, Rachel and Marcus were face to face once again.

At the entrance of Jackson Park, on that warmer-than-usual mid-morning in July, Marcus texted Ra-

chel to let her know he had arrived. Rachel climbed out
of her car in a light pink knee-length sundress, adjusted
her flat white canvas sneakers and placed her sun hat on
top of her black hair. Just before shutting her car door,
Rachel looked at herself in the reflection of her car
window, applied lip gloss and closed her door. Turning
around, in the not-so-far distance, she spotted Marcus
and instantly a smile stretched her face wide.

Making her way toward him she could see he was
dressed in light shorts hitting just above his knees leading her to notice his muscular legs, a T-shirt that fit his
body well enough to show that he hits the gym and
oddly enough she noticed he was wearing almost the
same style of shoe she was wearing. As he got closer to
her, she could see his teeth peeking through his lips exposing his happiness of seeing her again. He approached
her, and instantly pulled her in for a hug. Rachel was
mesmerized by not only the smell of his cologne, but
how deliberate his hug was. For a second as he held her
to his chest, Rachel clung to the feeling of safety his
arms and chest held. Marcus released Rachel from his
hug and the two made their way to the entrance of the
festival.

"You look amazing Rachel," Marcus said grabbing
Rachel's hand and spinning her around. As Rachel's
body twirled, her pink sundress did as well. Picking up
air Marcus noticed Rachel's toned legs and spun her
around again. Rachel laughed and as she began to lose
balance, Marcus pulled her in close and they walked
hand in hand toward the ticket taker standing outside
the makeshift silver barrier marking the entrance of the
festival. Rachel handed her tickets over to the young
man wearing a red and white gingham shirt and he led
them to their "picnic place." Rachel and Marcus took

their seats at picnic place #5. As they sat on the green and white checked blanket sponsored by Lovely Girls Café, they looked around and took it all in.

A field of picnic place settings covered the majority of Jackson Park, a different blanket representing each café or diner creating an amazing color pattern as far as they could see. Each set up with a take-home basket, plates, and silverware, some still empty and others occupied with ticket holders. Surrounding them were couples holding hands making their way to their places, kids running by and the chatter of anticipation for the festival to begin. A few dogs made their way by on leashes held by people happy to be right where they were in that moment. As the sun made its way higher, the smells of sunblock, baked pie, and comfort food got more intense and filled their nostrils to create a smell that would never be replicated.

Rachel and Marcus sat close. Marcus, curious about what was inside the basket, reached over, grabbed it and together they examined the contents. Gift certificates, T-shirts, and Koozies all with the logo of Lovely Girls Café on them. A welcome letter from the owners and a menu for the day's picnic were inside.

In the distance they heard music playing and saw they had a live band and then the announcement that the festival was about to kick off. Following the festival that would carry on into the evening, they were welcome to stay for the fireworks display and a night of dancing under the stars. Marcus placed his hand on Rachel's exposed skin on her leg and smiled at her. Rachel, smiling back, leaned her head on his shoulder. Hours later, after they enjoyed baked chicken, homemade mac'n cheese, marinated mushrooms, asparagus goat cheese salad, and conversations about jobs, family life, and previous dating experiences, they sat on the blanket and enjoyed a comfortable silence together and sipped on their raspberry lemonade rose coolers.

Rachel, her sunhat now resting on her stomach, leaned on Marcus's torso for a few minutes and listened to the surroundings. Marcus began to stroke her hair and Rachel fell into comfort instantly. As the band began to play, Rachel opened her eyes and sat up turning to look at Marcus. As their eyes met, Rachel leaned in and kissed Marcus. Slightly pulling away, Rachel saw the smile on his face, and she placed her hand on his stomach and kissed him again.

"So," Marcus began with Rachel now sitting beside him and the evening slowly turning into night, "what happened with your ex, Alex? You never really talked a lot about it," he said looking off toward the band in the distance and then toward Rachel, who was quiet.

"It was a hard relationship," she said softly. "I stayed too long in a place where I was no longer welcome. He was a nice guy, but like Sloane, he was selfish," she explained, still looking away from Marcus. "He cheated on me with the neighbor across the hall. She was younger than both of us and was tempted by his charms. I walked in on them. They both stayed frozen under the sheets as I put my engagement ring on the side table. I packed a small bag as they just stared at me waiting for me to react," she said now looking toward Marcus. "It was actually the best thing to happen to me. I was beginning to become more miserable with him each day. He lost his job, drank during the day, and started to call me names. So, when I saw them, I was relieved. No one would expect me to stay. No one would question why I left. If he had only lost his job, or was only drinking too much, I would have been labeled as not supportive, but a cheater? You are allowed to leave a cheater, but not a drunk," she said as Marcus grabbed her hand and squeezed it.

He leaned in and kissed her forehead. Rachel closed her eyes and let herself feel him close to her body. "Days after I left, Alex called and wanted to talk. I told him I would because I needed to get the rest of my stuff from his apartment. As he talked, I packed. I was calm and I listened to him, but as I was gathering my clothes, the door opened and Tabby from across the hall walked in. She had a key," Rachel said as she shook her head.

"Tabby. What an awful name," Marcus said, and they both laughed.

"It really is," agreed Rachel, "but that was it. I moved back in with my parents for a few months, saved up, and got my own place. Now I'm happy. My job keeps me busy, and I have friends I would be lost without. I have been putting off dating," she said as she forced her body to bump into his, "but I am glad I am here now," she said making eye contact with Marcus.

"Me too," Marcus said, "I'm glad to have met you, but I am sorry for your hurt," he said as he wrapped his arm around her.

In the distance the speaker came on announcing the festival was ending and the fireworks were set to begin in 30 minutes. As the band began to play after the announcements, Marcus and Rachel dropped their basket off at Rachel's car and made their way to the fireworks show.

Andrew Casper

A few days later after training with her coach and seeing her friends at Rachel's new place, Sydney got ready to go to the Baking/Pastry convention center. With her ticket ready to go, she got into her car, set her radio, and she was off. Although it wasn't too far, it was still an hour and a half ride to get there. While en route to the convention center, her phone rang. Piper's name came across the screen on her dashboard.

"Hey!" Sydney said happily.

"So, I was thinking," Piper said.

"No. Whatever it is, no. I already know it's a bad idea, so no. Actually, don't even say it," Sydney insisted.

"You know how Rachel is obviously still in love with Marcus?" she asked. "What if?" she began but Sydney cut her off.

"No, Piper. If Rachel wants to call him, she will. You have to let her make her own decisions," Sydney insisted.

"So, I just won't include you," Piper said, and then disconnected the call.

"Damn it Piper, always interfering," Sydney whispered as she turned her radio back on.

As she pulled up to the convention center, she had

no idea where she was supposed to park. There were no signs, so she just pulled into the nearest parking garage. She noticed there were not a lot of cars, so she was worried that either she was in the wrong place or possibly she had the wrong day.

She got out of the car and followed the signs to the elevator; the signs led her to the stairs. She walked down the stairs and as she turned to go down one more flight, not only did she see the elevator, but she saw Andrew. "Wait," she said to herself, "that looks like Andrew Casper from *America's Bake Off with Andrew Casper*. No, it couldn't be. Why would he be here," she thought to herself and then realized, "oh it's a baking convention. But he's an amazing baker?" She said confused and still not sure it was even really him.

He was standing alone in front of the elevator doors waiting for them to open. He heard her on the stairs and looked up at her. When their eyes met, they connected, and she was frozen. Honestly, she had not set eyes on a better-looking man since Daniel. That was him. That is him. Andrew Casper. She slightly shook herself out of the trance he unknowingly put her in and continued down the stairs. As she got closer, her stomach turned a bit and then he smiled. When he smiled, she lost it. With his full lips and bright white teeth, he lit up her world. Without saying a word, there was something. His dark skin, tight navy-blue polo type shirt that held onto his muscular biceps and was tucked into his professional looking pants and the shoes he was wearing matched his belt perfectly put him together in a perfect package. As she got closer to him, she could smell his cologne and the doors opened.

As he stood in front of the elevator, with a big welcoming smile on his face, he held the door and motioned for her to go in. She walked through the doors and felt numb, nervous. He walked in behind her, and as he went to press the button of the floor he wanted to go to, he looked at her and asked, "which floor?"

"Lower level, please," she said as she noticed he had already pressed the button with LL on it.

"Are you going to the convention?" he asked as the elevator began to move. "That's where I am headed."

"I am. I had no idea where to park. Either I am in the wrong place, or we are the only ones going to this," she said with an uncomfortable laugh.

"Yeah, I noticed that too actually," he said making eye contact with her and that same big bright smile on his face. As the elevator doors opened, he held the door open for her again and again, she walked through them. They walked together toward the convention and on the way, they made small talk.

"I am Andrew by the way," he said as he held out his hand toward Sydney.

"It's great to meet you Andrew, I'm Sydney," she said as she accepted the hand he was offering. The two held their handshake for a few seconds. As they made their way to the convention center, the conversation continued. She told him about The Lemon Bar and moving to Boston. He told her he was there visiting for the convention but was also looking for an apartment in the city. He explained about possibly recording his show in the city. As they walked in, they realized they were not the only ones there, but they had both parked in the wrong garage. They shared a laugh as they walked into the convention center and were greeted by a girl handing out an itinerary and map of the booth stations.

"I'm mostly here for the pastry demos," she said as she scanned the paper she was handed, "but the rest of this looks really interesting," she continued.

"I am here mostly as a guest on a panel," Andrew said, trying to get her attention back on him. "Be sure to put that on your itinerary."

Just as Sydney looked up from her map, she noticed a small crowd walking toward Andrew. As she looked past him over his shoulder, he turned around to see what she was looking at, and just like that Andrew was engulfed in a swarm of his fans. Sydney stood by for a second, and when Andrew didn't turn around, she walked away. As she was walking toward the demo area, she turned back to see him one last time, and when she did, she was surprised to see him looking back at her. She waved a little wave and he smiled big at her.

Sydney made her way around the convention center stopping at booths and picking up pamphlets and swag bags when she could. She tasted a few pastries and drank some of the wine that accompanied a few treats. After watching the demo on pastry shaping, she decided to call it a day. As she headed toward the same door that brought her into the convention center, she heard Andrew's voice booming from the panel he was a guest on. As she heard the crowd laugh, her stomach dropped a bit and she wasn't sure why, so she kept walking toward the door and eventually made her way back to her car.

A few days later, Sydney was back in her normal routine. One evening just as the bakery was closing, Sydney decided she would stay a bit later after closing to put to use some of the things she had learned during the demo she watched at the convention. In the kitchen, she grabbed her apron and as she tied it around her waist, she heard the chime of the door opening.

"Sorry, but we are closing," she called out as she

made her way to the front of the bakery. "Oh," she said, shocked. "Andrew, what, what are you doing here?" she asked both confused and a bit excited to see him standing in The Lemon Bar.

"Sydney. Hi. I found you! What happened to you the other day? I waited and looked for you during my panel. I was hoping to see you after and maybe get a drink with you," he said directly.

Sydney stood behind the counter in shock. Andrew Casper was in her bakery and said he wanted to have a drink with her. She stood there just looking at him trying to let what he just said sink in.

"Oh," she said blankly snapping herself out of her shock, she continued, "yeah, I had to go. I had to get home, but I heard the audience laughing at something you said as I was leaving."

"Are you busy now?" he asked, turning his head toward the front door. "It looks like you guys are closing in a few. How about we get a drink now? Or dinner if you are hungry?" he said nervously. "Are you hungry?"

"Yeah, yeah, I ah, I could eat," she said as she looked around the empty bakery to see if anyone could see Andrew Casper nervously asking her out, "I just need to close up and I can meet you right after?" she asked.

"That sounds great. I saw an Italian place a few doors down actually. Will that work for you?" he asked pointing his thumb to the left and putting it down as soon as he noticed he was pointing with his thumb.

"Yup. I will meet you there in say ten minutes?" she asked.

"Great! Yes. Ten minutes it is," he said as he turned to leave the bakery.

"Perfect," she said with a laugh and a blush for him. She could see how nervous he was and that made her feel calmer.

As soon as Andrew was out the door, Sydney rushed in the back, frantically ripping off her apron, rummaged through her handbag groping for her lipstick and her phone. She dialed Piper's number and as soon as Piper picked up, she went off.

"Piper! OMG. He's here. Andrew Casper is here. Andrew was at the convention center, and I met him in the elevator and now, he's here in The Lemon Bar. Well now he's a few doors down waiting for me. Waiting for me!! Me Piper, he wants to have dinner with me," she said all at once without breathing while checking her hair and applying lipstick.

"Wait, what? Andrew Casper? That hot guy from the baking show you force me to watch. That Andrew Casper?" she asked. "What? You met him? And now you are meeting him for a date? How did I not know you met him and why are you calling me and not sitting down with Andrew Casper?" she demanded. "Go Syd. Go now! But your ass better call me after!" she exclaimed.

Sydney stood in front of the prep table holding her phone in her hand. She placed the phone down on the table. She inhaled and then exhaled. Without thinking, she grabbed her bag, turned off the lights, and headed to the front door. Putting in the code for the security system and then locking the door, Sydney thought for one second about Daniel and made her way a few doors down to meet with Andrew Casper.

Seconds before Sydney opened the door to Valentino's Italian Café, she closed her eyes, opened them again, cleared her throat and made her way inside. In the back corner, she saw Andrew sipping a glass of red while looking over the menu. At that moment she appreciated the fact that he was not on his phone. A sign, to her, that he was confident sitting alone and she liked that. Andrew looked up and caught her eye. His smile widened the closer she got to the table and as she began to greet him, he stood up and pulled out her chair, but not before giving her a hello hug. Gentle and welcoming. Her face brightened and her smile widened as well.

As the two sat in the corner of Valentinos, others nearby could hear them laughing and talking. A few times the laughter from Sydney was so loud, others began to look at her. She noticed, but she didn't care and neither did Andrew. They drank and ate and then drank and ate again. By the time they knew it, they were the only two in the restaurant. When Andrew looked up, he noticed this. He looked toward the bar and saw the bartender drying glasses with a white cloth and he nodded his head toward Andrew, which Andrew took as "take your time," and that was his plan.

As the hours passed Sydney learned that Andrew had never married but wanted to one day. He also wanted kids. He loved his current life of travel and meeting new people, and he wasn't yet ready to settle down. Something Sydney understood because she also wasn't ready to settle down just yet. Andrew explained how things with his ex, Julia, didn't work out because she hated his travel and he felt pressure to get married. She also learned that Andrew learned to bake from his dad.

His dad owned a small bakery in the town he grew up in. His dad was somewhat famous, if you count the church and the book club ladies who were obsessed with his bread. His dad made birthday cakes for babies and years and years later he made wedding cakes for those same babies that were now getting married. Andrew inherited his passion from his dad, but his good looks from his mom, he joked.

As Andrew talked and listened, Sydney could not help but smile. She noticed how she was feeling as she sat with him. She was still. She was calm. She was happy. She enjoyed him and his stories and his laugh. She could listen to his laugh all day long if he would allow her to. As the conversation changed from Andrew and his life to Sydney's life, she knew what question was coming and she was not entirely prepared for it.

"So, what about you and your last relationship? Were you ever close to getting married? Is marriage something you are interested in?" he asked as he looked at her, sat back in his chair, crossed his legs, and sipped his wine.

Sydney held her wine glass. She looked in her glass as she swirled the red liquid around. She paused and then she spoke. When she spoke, she had Andrew's full attention. His facial expressions changed as she told him about Daniel, moving to Boston, and beginning her life again. After she told her story about Daniel, she expressed to him that she was unsure about marriage right now. Maybe in a few years or in a few months she would know how she felt about it, but for now, for tonight, she was unsure about her future plans. She knew at one point she wanted to marry Daniel, but she had no idea if she would or could ever feel that way about another man again. Andrew looked at Sydney when he felt she was finished speaking. He told her how he felt about her in that moment.

"You are so brave Sydney. I admire that about you."

Sydney smiled at him, held her arms across her chest and said nothing. A few minutes later Andrew looked at his watch and announced how late it was. The two got up and walked out of the restaurant and finished their first official date.

Eleven

Happy Birthday

Mid-September in Boston not only signified the beginning of fall, but it also meant Rachel's birthday was fast approaching. Although this birthday was not a significant one, it was cause for celebration, nonetheless. If you knew Rachel, you knew she loved her birthday. The last birthday she celebrated she was still with Marcus, and Marcus was not the birthday celebrator.

"But it's my birthday, we should go celebrate and have fun. Like a rooftop bar!" Rachel said excitedly.

"Rach, I love your birthday and how happy it makes you, but you know I have cases to go over. How about we order in and watch a movie, you pick. I promise I won't fall asleep," he negotiated.

Rachel looked at him disappointed. She knew he loved her, but she was sick of feeling disposable. "Okay, I'll make plans with my friends to go out then," she said sadly.

"Perfect," he said, kissing her on her forehead. Hours later he was fast asleep on the couch, and she was watching a documentary that he thought looked good.

"Listen," Rachel said. "This year for my birthday, I want to go out! I want glam and fun and drinks. Whatever you need to do to make that happen, you do it.

Got it?"

Sydney, Grace, and Piper started blankly at her from across the table.

"Okay Rachel, we can plan something," Grace said. "Do you want it to be a party or just a night out?" she asked.

"Surprise me," Rachel said. "I just want to dress up and be the star of the show."

Rachel was not always outgoing, but when it came to her birthday, she was a different person.

"Luckily, I have a few connections in the party planning world. I can make a few calls and see what we can do," Piper said.

"Thank you, Piper!" Rachel said with a big smile on her face.

"But," Piper continued, "we should talk about Marcus."

Sydney looked at Piper with a death stare.

"What?" Piper asked.

"Talk about him how?" Rachel asked.

"Should we invite him?" Grace asked.

"Guys, Rachel's birthday party is not the right time for a conversation like that to happen," Sydney said, "but it needs to happen," she added sipping on her drink.

"I have been thinking about it a lot more lately. I know I should reach out, but what if he's mad?" she asked.

"Oh, he's mad. He's for sure mad. But you sort of made this mess, Rach, now you need to clean it up," Grace said.

Although she was right, her words hit Rachel in the gut.

"I'll think about it, but in the meantime, let's get on

these party plans!" Rachel said feeling as if she wanted to throw up but pretended to not feel anything with Grace's words.

"How is everyone else doing? How's Dax?" Rachel asked.

"Yeah, have you heard from Cory since seeing him with Dax?" Piper asked.

During the weeks after meeting him, Grace was getting used to Daxton. His morning texts, his daily coffee selfies on his way to work, the way he kissed her. Those were just a few of the things she grew accustomed to as she began to build something with Daxton. She was not sure what it was exactly, but she looked forward to him. Seeing him, hearing from him. Just him. One late afternoon days after running into Cory, as Grace was leaving work, her phone buzzed. She reached for her phone and saw a familiar face across her screen. With a look of confusion, she took the call.

"Cory? Is everything okay?" she asked, slightly concerned. She had not seen or heard from him since she and Daxton ran into him at the coffee shop.

"Hi Grace. Yeah, yeah everything is okay. I was calling to check in on you. To…. see how you were. How are you? Everything good?" he asked in the same suave voice she had been used to hearing for so many years.

"I'm great actually, I am just leaving work now. It was really good to see you a few weeks ago. I was a bit shocked and hadn't expected to run into you. I mean it makes sense because we both live close by, but I didn't expect it," she replied.

"Yeah, I didn't expect it either. I knew at some point this would happen, but I didn't think I would see you with someone else," he slightly hesitated as his words dripped out of his mouth.

"Yeah, I know. It was odd for me as well," she said.

"So, who is he? Is it serious?"

"Well, this is an unusual conversation to have right now, but I am not sure if it's serious yet. I just met him a few weeks ago. Actually, I met him a few days before I saw you." Without knowing why, in that moment, she felt comfortable talking to Cory about Daxton. So, she continued, "I didn't expect to meet him. It was sort of random, but right away I felt something with him. He's so charming. He reaches out to me. He told me how comfortable he feels with me, and he says he trusts me already. He has never trusted someone so fast or as much as he trusts me. He checks in and likes to talk to me. He even says he wants to get married someday." She now found herself sitting in her car with a smile on her face realizing she has deep feelings for him already.

"Sounds sort of fast to me Grace. How much do you really know about this guy? I didn't like how he sort of dragged you out of the coffee shop when I saw you," he said, concerned.

"Cory, he's just protective," Grace said, suddenly frustrated, "he didn't want me to feel uncomfortable seeing you and I am glad he did that. It really was uncomfortable seeing you unexpectedly. What he did was actually very sweet!" she rubbed her arm where the bruise Daxton left was just about gone. "I have to go, Cory. It was good talking to you," she hung up on him before he could respond.

Grace sat in her parked car for a few minutes after hanging up. "Was he jealous? Why would he say something like that?" she asked out loud to no one. She sat back, still holding her bruised arm and thought back to that day. Then, coming to the realization that Daxton really likes her, she shook herself out of it because he

The Wedding | 91

was truly trying to keep her safe, she reasoned.

Piper, Rachel, and Sydney sat in silence looking at each other for a moment.

"Have you talked to him since?" Piper asked knowing the email she requested for the guest list was in her inbox waiting for her.

"No, I don't need his negative energy around me," Grace said.

"When do we get to meet Daxton?" Sydney asked. "Maybe Rachel's party?"

"I will invite him. We have been having fun together," she said.

"Are you spending much time with him? What's he like?" Rachel asked.

Grace and Daxton began to see each other more often. They met up when they could, and he would sleep at her place because he said his place was "unfit" for a woman to sleep in; plus, he liked Grace's place and the location. It was clear across town, and he liked the variety of bars and restaurants that he would mostly order takeout from when he was staying with her. While together they would head a few cities over to visit museums and see musicals and dramas at the Paramount.

Daxton took her on a sailing cruise around the Mystic River. As they boarded the sailboat, she was greeted with champagne and a sunset picnic. Grace swooned after that amazing night and with the temperature changing Daxton and Grace went apple picking at a farm a few hours away. While there, they made a scarecrow and carved pumpkins into jack-o'-lanterns, which sat on the small balcony of Grace's apartment until the pumpkins began to rot and the scarecrow was picked apart by bird.

Grace loved spending time with Daxton, but it

seemed whenever they went out, it was always somewhere a few hours away. After expressing her desire to
start going out in the city she loved, he explained that
he liked the time they spent together on their road trips,
but that he would make it a point to go out locally with
her.

One night as they sat outside on a restaurant patio
beneath the sky full of stars and a breeze in the air,
Daxton opened up to her about his past relationship.
She remembered how it felt the night he told her how
easy she was to talk to, how no one else had ever made
him feel this happy, how other girls were so difficult.
He told her about Charlotte, his ex. She was controlling
and never let him have his own life. He noted how she
would check his phone and call him all night long
while he was out with friends. He went on to explain
how she never took care of him while he was sick, the
house was never clean, and she never cooked for him.
She would make herself dinner and he would have to
get something delivered. As he recounted his history
with his ex, Grace hurt for him.

"I have feelings for you Grace," he said, making direct eye contact with her as he grabbed her hand which
she slid into his. "I am just not ready right now to go
public with anyone. Can I see us being together long
term? Yes. But right now, I just need time to figure
some stuff out on my end." He noticed her looking
down and then away from him. He grabbed her chin
and guided her to look in his direction. "Grace, I want
to be with you. I don't want you to be with anyone else.
I need you to be patient with me, okay?" he demanded
more than asked.

Looking up at him and into his blue eyes, she felt
his hand on her chin and he moved his chair closer to
her, their legs now touching. She reasoned within her-

self that although she would not wait too much longer, she would for now.

"Okay Dax. I can do that," she said, somewhat against her better judgement. But then she immediately felt the need to be strong for him, and that was what she was going to do. He was such a sweet guy who deserved so much better, and she was going to give him better if he allowed her to do so.

A week or so later, Grace was lost in thought at work while sitting at her desk when her phone buzzed. It was Daxton. With a sigh of relief and excitement, she picked up his call. She had not heard much from him in the past few days which was unusual. Lately she noticed him drifting off a bit. Normally she would hear from him in the morning on his way to work, along with calls or texts during the day, and she was getting used to seeing him a few times a week. But lately, all of that died down. When she picked up the phone, he said he only had a few minutes before he had to go to a dinner meeting. With those few minutes she had, she asked him if things were okay between them. He answered by saying he was sorry he was so busy and he promised they were okay. Grace felt better, but also felt as if something was off.

A few hours later when Grace was home in her apartment, the doorbell rang. She opened the door to find Daxton on the other side holding a bottle of wine from the winery they had visited and a pizza box from the new pizza place they talked about trying. She stopped in her tracks for a moment and took him in while he stood in the doorway. His face was so pleasing to the eye, his stature was great and his eyes gleamed. As she looked at him and he began to walk in, her stomach filled with butterflies, and she knew her feelings for him were turning to love.

The Wedding Date

"So as far as a wedding date goes, what are you thinking?" she asked him as they both pulled out their calendars.

"Let's first pick a season, then a month and go from there?" he asked.

"When I was younger, I wanted a June wedding, but now I am thinking November or February. If we did February, we could do winter wonderland theme," she said excitedly.

He looked at her from the across the couch and he felt so happy to see her lighting up talking about the date.

"I can do a winter wonderland theme," he said with a smile.

"Yeah?" she asked, "okay let's look at the dates, but we need to look further than just the wedding date, we have to consider our anniversaries too. Like if we do February, will we be able to travel because of the weather? You know?" she said.

"Good point baby," he said.

"So can we do something in the winter and not fear the weather for the next, oh I don't know 100 or so years?" she asked with a giant smile on her face.

"Well let's see, November is usually not too wintery, if you know what I mean, we can still get away with the theme you like," he said looking at his calendar on his phone.

"When I hear November wedding though, I think

golds and pumpkins, not winter blue. November is great, but not for the theme," she said.

"Are you stuck on this theme?" he questioned.

"I'm not sure," she said looking him with a confused look on her face. "What other options do we have?"

After looking at other opinions, fall, spring, summer, farmhouse, destination, they made a decision.

"Let's do February and stick with the winter wonderland theme. I know it can be risk for anniversaries, but this is the date we are going to become one, and if we need to postpone a trip or celebration because of weather, well there is no one I would rather do that with," he said looking at her.

"Really? If you are sure, lets pick the date!" she said happily beaming.

After comparing calendars with work events, social gatherings, and everything in between, they settled on...

February 12

Twelve

It's THE Gown

"Hello?" Rachel said sleepily into her phone, looking at the time.

"Happy Birthday!!!" the voice yelled.

"Thank you?" she said not recognizing the voice on the other end.

"It's time to get up, eat something and get showered, we will be picking you up in two hours!"

"Piper?" Rachel asked.

"Obviously. We have your birthday plans, and they are ready to go, now get up," and she was gone.

Rachel laid in her bed trying to wake and she wondered what kind of plans Piper made for her big day.

"Twenty-nine," she said under her breath and her peaceful room was interrupted by her phone ringing again.

"Hey Dad," she said sleepily again.

"Happy Birthday Sweetie!" he said happily.

"Thanks Dad, how are you?" she asked still feeling groggy.

"I'm good, your mom is good, you know how it is. Oh, she said she will call you later, she had plans for breakfast this morning, you know how she loves to be up early and loves me to be up early too." you could hear the irritation in his voice as he spoke.

"Hey kid, so have you talked to Marcus at all?" he asked knowing this question was like a landmine.

"Why is everyone asking about Marcus?" she thought to herself

"No Dad, I haven't. Why?"

"There is something I should have told you a year ago but didn't" he began as her stomach dropped. "After you left; he came by the house."

"What?" she sat up in bed, throwing the covers off. "What?" she said again.

"It was few days after you left. He called and then came by. When I opened the door, he was a mess. He was upset, said he could not get in touch with you, and he asked me if you were okay," he paused and when Rachel didn't say anything, he continued, "I told him you would reach out when you were ready, that you just needed time. He didn't quite understand, but he accepted what I said. He wanted to know your new number, but I thought it best to just let it be." He sat still and quiet for a minute more and when she still didn't say anything, he began to speak again. "You know, he's a good guy, Rach. I know he messed up; I know he did. But I have talked to him recently and I think you should call him." he said.

"I have to go Dad. I love you." and she disconnected the call. In her bed she rolled over onto her stomach and screamed into her pillow until her throat hurt.

After a few minutes, she gathered herself and her heavy mind, made her way to the kitchen and eventually she got into the shower.

Two hours later there was loud knocking at her front door. When she opened it balloons were shoved in her face and confetti was flying through the air.

"It's birthday time!" Piper shouted, and the others followed in behind her.

Although Rachel loved the birthday attention, she pondered telling her friends about Marcus. In an instant, she decided against it and threw herself into birthday mode.

"Yes! Thank you, guys, so much! So, what is the plan? You didn't tell me what to wear so I dressed casually," she explained in her jeans and T-shirt.

"No worries, this is exactly what you should be wearing." Grace said as she grabbed Rachels handbag, and they began to lead her to the door.

"Oh, so we are leaving?" Rachel asked confused.

"Yep, let's get in the car and go!" Sydney said as she shut the door behind them.

A few left turns and another right turn and they were outside of an unmarked building. Piper parked her car out front.

"Um, what are we doing here exactly?" Rachel asked nervously.

"It's a surprise," Grace said, laughing, "don't worry, you will be safe."

The friends got out of the car and headed toward the door. Just as they got close, Louis, Piper's newest and most influential client at TOGETHER, opened the door.

Louis was dressed in a black suit with a pink bedazzled tie. His shoes matched his tie, and he was wearing a giant smile on his face.

"Piper," he said exaggerating her name, "so good to see you, my love," and he kissed her on both cheeks.

"Don't you look fabulous on this beautiful day," Piper responded.

"Piper," he said playfully scolding, "Peter did not

work out last night. He was absolutely terrible."

"Louis, I promise I will find you someone amazing." she said to her newest match-making high-end client.

"Okay girl, I will hold you to that. Alright let's see," he said, scanning her friends and softly clapping his hands together. "Where is my birthday girl?"

Rachel hesitantly raised her hand and Louis made his way to her and grabbed her hand. As he led her through the metal doorway, the group followed. On the other side of the door Rachel was surprised to see a photo shoot set up. Upon further inspection, Rachel discovered it was a birthday shoot.

"Well, what do you think?" Piper asked as they all looked at Rachel.

Rachel looked around the warehouse that was spacious except for a small area that had a pink backdrop, next to a few giant cupcakes, candles, and birthday hats. Next to them she could see a make-up and hair crew unpacking and getting ready. Beyond the makeup artists' set up were racks of gowns, shoes, and accessories. Without speaking, Louis lead the group to hair and make-up.

"This is for me?" Rachel asked confused.

"Yes! It's a surprise birthday photo shoot," Piper said as she linked arms with Rachel. "I wanted to make this one special, so I called in a few favors."

"Looks like more than a few," Rachel said looking at Piper. "Thank you, and I really mean that. This is incredible."

"Don't get too excited," Grace said, "we have a few more surprises headed your way today," she said as they made themselves comfortable in the hair and make-up chairs. They put their coffee down, hung their handbags on the back of the chairs and looked at themselves in the mirror.

"So, you all look like a tight knit group of friends. How did you come to find each other?" Louis asked as he began to brush out Piper's hair.

"We have all been friends a while now. Piper and I met in the third grade," Grace began.

"Yeah, that was the day when Pete Linkmore dripped ice cream on Grace at lunch table 9," Piper said specifically.

"Yeah, and then Piper stood up for me after he called me a bitch, and she made him apologize in front of everyone," Grace continued, "We have been inseparable since then, including going to Bowdoin together after high school."

"Yeah, we have made it all this way as best friends," Piper added.

"Those college stories are for another day though," Grace said as they all laughed.

"How did the rest of you meet?" Louis asked continuing to brush out Piper's hair.

"Piper and I met in a random way actually. I was sitting in a hole-in-the-wall burger place close to my new apartment, a few days after I moved to Boston, and as I was busy on my phone, I heard the familiar sounds of the doorbell chime. When I looked up, I saw a face I knew but for the life of me, I could not place it. I looked at him, and the woman he was with, and could not place either of them. But after a few minutes I heard someone calling my name. Turns out Curt, the man Piper was with, went to school with my fiancée Daniel." She paused. "He has since passed away. But I invited them both to sit with me, and we have been friends ever since. What ever happened to Curt?" Sydney asked looking toward Piper.

"You know, I am not sure," Piper said, and they laughed. "Rachel and I met in a cycling class."

"Okay, so a totally embarrassing moment in my life," Rachel began. "As I climbed on to a bike, the seat fell off. You know how you are in a new class and suddenly you feel as if you are on display? Well, that was me. Piper hopped of her bike and helped me out," Rachel said, grabbing Piper's hand and then Grace and Sydney stood behind them. "I would have been lost if I didn't meet these incredible women," Rachel said.

"Okay birthday girl!" Louis called out, "let's get you into a gown and get this shoot poppin'.s" Rachel got up and headed toward him with her glass in hand and a smile clear across her face.

"Guys!" Rachel yelled as she pulled apart the faux dressing room door, "what do you think?"

Rachel appeared in a black, long sleeve, floor length, floral embroiled Oscar de la Renta velvet lace gown that hugged her fit, toned body.

"OMG," Piper said.

"Damn," Grace said with her jaw on the floor.

"You look incredible Rachel," Sydney said.

"I feel amazing," Rachel said as she made her way towards them with a spin.

Minutes later all four friends stood in front of the pink backdrop and posed for pictures together. They added in the giant cupcakes and as they posed with them, they laughed and grabbed the candles. Wearing birthday hats and holding balloons, someone in the back began to sing happy birthday. The photographer yelled out "fun pose" and confetti fell from the ceiling.

While in Piper's car, as they made their way to Hotel Fade, they discussed how fun the shoot was, what to do with the pictures and what the rest of the day held.

"What's the plan for the rest of the day?" Rachel asked excitedly.

"We are headed to Hotel Fade and sending you to the spa for a birthday massage and then we are having a small dinner at Whiskeys," Grace said with a smile as she looked at Rachel.

"Damn, you guys are going all out for me," Rachel said sweetly.

"We love you Rach," Piper said, looking at her in her rearview mirror.

A few hours later, after they'd sent Rachel to the hotel spa and to get ready for her surprise party later that night, Piper closed the door of the hotel suite and gathered Grace and Sydney on the couch in their sitting area.

"Okay guys, I did something," Piper said excitedly.

Sydney's heart sank in fear.

"What," Sydney said coldly.

"I called Marcus," Piper said, covering her mouth with her hands.

"No. No you did not," Sydney said.

"I did. And we talked. I told him Rachel may be willing to talk to him."

Sydney stood up and faced Piper.

"You had no right to do that. No right!" Sydney said with an elevated voice. "Who do you think you are always medaling in other people's lives? It is none of your business what Rachel does and who she does it with, Piper. You crossed a line."

"I didn't cross a line Syd. Rachel misses him, you can see it on her face when she talks about him."

"It does not matter Piper!" Sydney interrupted. "You had no right," Sydney stood with her hand on her head. "Please tell me you didn't tell him about the party tonight," She asked

Piper sat still, looked at Sydney and didn't say a word.

"You told him. Is he coming?" Grace asked.

"Maybe," Piper said.

"Great," Sydney said, "just great."

"The most important thing we need to know is if he is coming tonight. If he is, we need damage control," Sydney said. "Rachel misses him, but she is not ready to talk to him yet, you had no right."

"Okay Syd, we get it, but what is done is done. Piper, is he coming tonight?" Grace asked.

"I don't know," Piper responded.

"What did he say?" Sydney asked.

"He said he was happy that I called, and he wanted to see her. I didn't give him any information about her except that her party was tonight. He said he would think about going and let me know," Piper explained.

"So now we just wait and see if he shows up?" Grace asked as she sighed.

"Yep, looks that way," Sydney said in a snarky tone.

"I thought I was doing something good," Piper tried to explain.

"Well next time, just let others decide what they want in their lives," Sydney said. "I'm going to shower and get ready."

Thirteen

Piper Invited Me

To say Rachel was surprised would be an understatement. After getting back to her room from her massage, she walked in to find an overly large gold box with a silver sparkly bow wrapped around it. Looking at the box confused, she picked up the note beneath the bow.

Dear Rachel,

You were stunning today; you deserve to look this beautiful today and every day! See you tonight!

xx Louis

Rachel opened the box to find a beautifully framed picture of her and her friends from the day's shoot, and under the photo, wrapped in tissue paper, was the dress she wore for her photo shoot.

"OMG!" she exclaimed. "Guys!" she yelled to her friends. "Get in here!"

As her friends ran to her room, they found Rachel holding the dress in her hands and tears filling her eyes.

"Happy Birthday Rachel!" they said in unison and popped a bottle of champagne.

Hours later, with Rachel dressed in her Oscar de la Renta, she celebrated her 29th birthday with her friends and family in the event room at Paintings, a new luxury restaurant in the Seaport District.

The room, decorated in black and gold, held about 100 people including Rachel's dad who drove in for the occasion. Around the room Rachel saw not only her mom, dad and Louis who put the party together, but her friends from home, work, and even a few from her spin class.

"This truly was a surprise," Rachel told her dad as they stood under a ceiling covered in balloons. "I feel so loved right now," she continued.

"You have met some really great friends, Rachel. They really love you," he said with a smile on his face as he looked at his daughter. "You deserve some happiness. I'm sorry if I upset you this morning talking about Marcus."

"Marcus?" Liz, Rachel's mom was confused. "What about Marcus?" she looked around the room holding her glass of red wine. "Is he here?"

Rachel's dad once again put his foot in his mouth. "No Liz, he's not here," he said as he linked arms with his wife to pull her aside to fill her in.

"Where are your parents going?" Sydney asked.

"My dad told me this morning that after I left Marcus, he came looking for me. I had no idea." She sipped her drink. "I was so confused this morning, but for now I need to just forget about him, and I can deal with this tomorrow. I guess he did not tell my mom either," she said looking their way. She could see that her mom was upset with her dad.

Sydney's stomach dropped. She looked around the room and wondered if Marcus would show up. As she looked, she realized she had no idea what he looked like. Just as she began to scan the room for the second time, the DJ began to play music.

"Ladies and gentlemen," the booming voice said over upbeat music, "welcome to Rachel's twenty-ninth birthday bash! Let's welcome the birthday girl to the center of the room," he finished, and lights scanned the room for Rachel.

She made her way to the center of the room and came face to face with her birthday cake. A four-tier, rainbow-frosted cake with sparklers shooting out of it.

The crowd sang.

After the candles were blown out, slices were devoured, and the party was getting started, Grace saw a familiar face in the crowd.

"Cory?" she asked as she approached him.

"Hey Grace," he said and went in for a hug.

Grace stepped back in surprise.

"What are you doing here?" she questioned but also noticed how good he looked. His blond hair looked like it was just cut, his blue eyes a bit shinier against his light blue shirt that hugged his body.

"Piper invited me. I thought she told you?" he said.

"Piper," she said under her breath, "of course. No, she didn't say anything to me," Grace said as she searched the room for Piper.

"Are you here alone?" Cory asked as he sipped his drink, making eye contact with her.

"Yes, Dax was supposed to be here, but he was called out of town unexpectedly," she said matter of factly, "so, I am on my own tonight."

"How is all of that going with him?" he asked.

"Great actually," she lied. "He's been nothing short of amazing," she lied again.

In reality, Daxton was confusing her. One day he was available and the next he was MIA. She had no idea why, but it was bothering her. When she asked about it, he always said the same thing, work. She understood work can be crazy, but he had mood swings and at times his phone would be off, and he held no answer as to why. He avoided certain subjects and Grace just let him because she had feelings for him.

"That's great, you look happy Grace," he lied as well.

Grace caught Piper's eye and she aggressively made her way toward her, leaving Cory standing alone.

"Piper," Grace demanded her attention.

"Hey Grace," Piper said cheerfully with a big smile on her face, thinking Grace would be happy with her.

"What the fuck Piper?" Grace sneered. "Why is he here? You know I'm with Daxton. Damn it Piper you are overstepping so many boundaries right now. Stay out of other people's lives," Grace sneered through her teeth and walked off leaving Piper stunned.

Sydney walked over concerned. "What just happened?" she asked.

"I think I did something bad," Piper said as she pulled Sydney off to the side.

"Okay I found something out about Daxton and have no idea what to do with it, so instead of telling Grace, I invited Cory in hopes he would distract her," Piper explained.

"What did you find out?" Sydney asked and just as Piper was about to tell her, Andrew walked up behind them holding three drinks.

"Hey. What's the huddle all about here?" he asked, noticing they looked out of place.

"Thanks so much for the drinks," Sydney said looking at Andrew with wide eyes. Rachel's party was the event where all the guys were supposed to meet the group. Andrew was the only one who was able to show up.

"Thanks," Piper said to Andrew as he handed her a drink.

"Everything okay?" he asked, concerned.

"Piper found something out about Daxton. Instead of telling Grace, she invited Cory to the party," Sydney explained to Andrew.

"Syd!" Piper said.

"What? He was going to find out either now or tonight," Sydney said as the two stood closer and giggled a bit.

"Cory?" Andrew asked. "That dude in the blue shirt? He's great. We talked for a while." Andrew said pausing to sip his drink.

"Okay," Piper said, "he can stay."

Andrew looked at Sydney and raised his eyebrows at her. "The inner circle," he said gleefully.

"Anyway, remember when I was going to get the guest list for the TOGETHER event where Grace met Daxton? Well, I got the venue list too. I made a call to the cousin, and he told me that Daxton was engaged."

Andrew spit his drink out.

"What?" he exclaimed.

"Engaged? To who?" Sydney said a bit too loud.

"A woman named Charlotte. A travel writer for *Travel Today*. She works remote a lot. Apparently, after they get married, she's going to cut back and try for kids," she explained. "They are supposed to be getting married soon. I'm not sure when, but does that really matter? What should we do?" Piper asked. "She's so mad at me right now. She won't listen to anything I tell her about him. For some reason she's in this trance over him."

"You know, the travel thing makes sense. She is always saying how he's here and then not. That would explain his mood swings and being 'called into work' for tonight." They all nodded their heads in agreement.

"Where is your new guy tonight?" Andrew asked.

"You tell him everything?" Piper asked Sydney.

"Yeah, sort of," she responded, "but good point, Andrew, where is he?"

"Well," she said, blushing, "he's supposed to be here soon," Piper said just as her phone buzzed.

Piper looked at them and said, "the doctor is here." In that moment, with Piper's back to the door and excitement on their faces, her friends all looked up and waited for him to walk in.

Through the door and with what looked like a gust of wind, Rand made an appearance. He stepped in and looked for Piper. As he looked around, someone asked him if he needed help finding someone. The friends watched as he was pointed in their direction, and they were able to get a better look at the tall, dark, over-the-top handsome stranger that had their once sad friend now smiling.

Walking toward them, Rand began to peel off layers of his fall outerwear. First came off the scarf, a green and black plaid accessory that matched his black waisted length peacoat that he was now beginning to unbutton, revealing his white T-shirt and neatly settled pine green V-neck sweater. With his coat off and firmly on his arm, and a smile exposing his perfectly straight white teeth, he approached the group.

"Hi," he said as he looked at Piper and then around at everyone else. He made eye contact with Piper again and his smile widened. Piper introduced Rand to the others.

"Rand, this is Sydney, her boyfriend Andrew, Grace, and Rachel, the birthday girl, is somewhere celebrating," Piper said looking to see if she could see Rachel.

"It's great to meet you all," Rand said smiling.

Just as they were about to get back to the party, Rachel walked up looking pale.

"Guys," she said looking at the triangle they created.

"Are you okay? You look like you have seen a ghost," Sydney said.

Piper's stomach dropped, remembering Marcus could possibly show up tonight.

"You are not going to believe who is here," Rachel said.

Asking The Bridesmaids

"How did it go?" he asked as she stumbled through the door.

"Great," she said, throwing herself on the couch.

He got up and made his way toward her. Laughing he asked, *"Did you have fun?"*

"Yep. And they said yes!" She threw her arms up and her hands were in fists.

"Are you able to tell me about it?" he asked.

"Well," she said trying to sit up, *"I went to the bar, gave the bartender the glasses that asked them each to be my bridesmaid and then ordered shots. When they came, they were against shots, but I made them take them,"* she said trying to not sound drunk, *"so, we took the shots, and no one noticed. Until they did. They were very excited."*

"That's great. I had no doubts they would easily accept," he said.

"Then we had more shots and drinks and not a lot of food," she said realizing she was hungry.

"I expected that," he said and walked into the kitchen. Minutes later he emerged with a grilled cheese sandwich and apple juice.

"OMG. This. This is why I am marrying you. You are the sweetest man ever," she gushed and sat up to eat.

"I love you," she said with a mouth full of cheese and bread.

"I love you too," he said smiling at her.

Fourteen

Opening Up

The next morning Sydney woke up next to Andrew. She grabbed her pillow, put it underneath her, and laid her head on it so she could look him. He was so peaceful while he slept, but he was also peaceful when he was awake too. She took in all of his features. His long lashes, his tight jaw, his dark skin, and his smooth bald head made him so attractive. She trusted him; she was realizing. She trusted him in the physical sense, but she also trusted him to take care of her heart and her emotions. She thought back to when they met, and she opened up about Daniel.

"It's okay Andrew. I am okay to talk about it," Sydney said as she herself could not believe she was going to talk about losing Daniel to a man she not only just met but felt this strong connection to.

In an instant, she realized that this was what she may have needed in order to move past it. She spoke about how she met Daniel, got together, and how they were planning on moving in together. Andrew listened intently and held her hand softly. Sydney went on about them being together for almost two years and as she talked about him, she looked happy. How happy they were together and how they got through their first fight.

But then her face changed. She became sadder.

"I was in bed one night. I stayed at Daniel's apartment on the days he worked his 48-hour shift at the firehouse. The phone rang, and somehow it made its way into my dream. Then it began to ring again and this time it woke me up. I sat up in his bed and grabbed my phone. I recognized the number; it was the firehouse. As soon as I saw it, my stomach dropped, my skin got hot, and I could feel tears rushing to my eyes. I knew it was bad news," she said, looking off into the distance. "There was a fire. Daniel went in but didn't come out. As he was making his way through the smoke trying to find the exit, part of the ceiling caved in, and he was blocked from leaving." Sydney inhaled and then exhaled and at the same time she felt Andrew squeeze her hand tighter.

Sydney paused for a moment and realized she felt better. She felt at ease. Feeling this way has not come easy for her and she was relaxed. After her pause she continued. "That was over a year and a half ago. The pain is still fresh, and it still hurts. I could not live in the town we lived in together anymore. So, I bought a bakery here in Boston, found a great apartment and made the move," she explained.

She felt Andrew stir next to her and she snapped out of her memory. Thinking he was waking up, Sydney turned her head to face the wall. But after realizing he was just adjusting, she rolled back over and looked at him again, she thought about how their relationship had developed mostly though long distance. With Andrew traveling for work, making guest appearances on baking TV shows, and Sydney working at The Lemon Bar, the two made time to really get to know each other, mostly via the phone. For the first few months things were difficult with Andrew still living long distance. But now that he was planning to move to Boston permanently, they could socialize more, and her friends could get to know him better.

"Good morning," Andrew whispered in his morning voice, "are you looking at me while I sleep, you creeper," he said as he opened his eyes.

"Yep," she said with a smile.

They got up and sat in the kitchen while the coffee maker brewed the coffee, and they began to unpack the previous night.

As they began to talk, Sydney's phone rang.

"Hey Rachel, you okay?" she asked.

"Yeah, I'm okay. Any chance you can meet for breakfast?"

"Yeah, Andrew has a taping in a bit, so I'm free," Sydney said.

"Great see you in thirty at The Usual," and she hung up

"That was weird," Sydney said to Andrew.

"Yeah, I bet she has feelings about last night," he said as he poured two cups of coffee.

As Sydney said goodbye to Andrew and they made plans to meet when he was back in town in a few weeks, she called Grace.

"Hey, are you meeting us at The Usual?" Sydney asked Grace when she answered her call.

"Yeah, I'm on my way now. Any idea what this is about? Rachel never calls us to brunch on her own," Grace asked.

"No idea, but I can't wait to find out. Why do I feel as if we are in trouble?" Sydney laughed. But she really felt that way.

Sydney, Grace, and Piper all walked into The Usual at the same time. Grace giving Piper a dirty look, she walked by her and found a seat near the window.

"Everything okay?" Piper asked Rachel.

"No. Not really. First, I want to thank you guys for last night. I had the best birthday ever. We made so many memories, but there is something going on in this group and it's not okay." She paused. "Secrets. There are secrets here and we need to get everything out in the open." She looked at Piper.

"What?" Piper asked.

"Let's talk about you inviting Cory behind my back," Grace shot her words at Piper as if they were daggers.

"Okay, I should not have done that. I was wrong, but I did want to tell you about some information I found out about Daxton," she said, and they all looked at Grace.

"What now, Piper?" Grace said, annoyed, as she folded her arms.

Piper inhaled deeply, and for a second thought carefully about her next words to her best friend. She knew she needed to say something but wasn't in the habit of breaking hearts. Piper closed her eyes and began to speak.

"Grace. As you know, I requested to see the guest list from the night you met Daxton. Well, a few days ago I found it buried deep in my emails. I looked it over and his name was not on it. So, I dug a little more."

Grace interrupted, "I know, Piper. He wasn't on the guest list because he was there with his cousin who was catering that night. Geez, why can't you just be happy for me?" Her tone had an annoyed and frustrated edge to it.

Piper continued, "So I called his cousin, the caterer, and he told me something about Daxton."

"What? Why? Why would you do something like that? You totally crossed the line! Why are you checking up on me? Do not treat me like a baby who can't handle her own life!" Grace practically yelled at her.

Although Piper knew how upset Grace was becoming, she told her what she had found out about Daxton. She knew there was a chance she may not believe her, but she had to try anyway.

"He's engaged!" Piper let out.

There was a minute of stunned silence.

"What? Dax is engaged. To who? No. He's not. He's my boyfriend," she started with a bit of sadness and shock in her voice.

"Her name is Charlotte. They have been together for three years and are engaged. His cousin told me when I called him."

"Oh my God!" Grace said as she began to laugh. "You nearly had me there. Charlotte is his ex. She was crazy. Dax told me all about her. Geez you need to get your information from a reliable source."

"Okay Grace. I told you what I needed to tell you, but you have to consider all possibilities. He is hit or miss. He's not very reliable. He calls mostly while he's at work, you have never been to his place and communication is not as strong as it was."

"Well, it's certainly not because he's engaged! That's insane! He is just busy, and things will settle down soon," Grace explained.

"Okay. Well, I just wanted to let you know what I heard. I hope I am wrong with this," Piper said.

"Why was Cory there last night?" Grace asked.

"Yeah," Rachel said. "When I saw him, I was shocked

and confused, but it was nice to see him again."

"I didn't want to tell you this about Dax, so I invited Cory so maybe you would miss him and want to be with him again," Piper admitted.

"Wow. So, you are giving me misinformation about Dax, and you are trying to trick me? Wow Piper. Just wow," Grace said, annoyed.

"Think about it Grace. He is always busy. He goes missing for days. And he never comes to events. Why is that?" Rachel asked. "And if you say he's busy, I'll scream. Married people with kids make time for affairs, so he can make time for you."

"Is there anything else Piper needs to admit today?" Grace said, throwing Piper under the bus.

Sydney looked at Grace and then at Piper, "Well, Piper, anything else?" Grace said as they all looked at Rachel.

"Oh no. What did you do?" Rachel asked Piper.

Fifteen

Going Home

Outside the cool air was surrounding her. She stood on the street just outside of her office building holding her cellphone in her hand by her side. As she stood in the heavy fall air, tears built up behind her eyes. She looked off into the distance at nothing. With the sounds of the city all around her, the horns, sirens, and hustle and bustle of people shopping, sightseeing, and rushing by, Piper felt tears running down her cheeks. She wiped them away and came out of her trance. She turned around and made her way back to her office on the top floor. As she approached the glass door that read TOGETHER, she heard someone saying her name. She turned around and saw her boss standing behind her.

"Piper. Are you okay?" Stephanie asked.

"It's my mom," Piper said blankly. "The hospital just called. She's there now. She couldn't stop throwing up and when the doctor looked at her scan..." Piper paused and suddenly ran to the bathroom.

"Piper, are you okay in there?" Stephanie asked even though she heard Piper throwing up.

"Sorry Stephanie," Piper said sitting on the floor in the first bathroom stall. "My mom has a brain tumor," she said slowly, and Stephanie could tell she choked those words out of her mouth. "I need to go home. In-definitely," Piper said as she trailed off.

Now sitting at her desk, Piper stared at her phone blankly, and then she called Rand. When he didn't answer, she sent a message to call her back as soon as he could. She told him in the message she had to go home for her mom. Although their relationship was in a sort of holding pattern, it was still there, but not much progress was made. But when she heard the news of her mom, that is who she wanted to call. She wasn't sure if it was because it was him, or because he was a neurosurgeon. Either way, she wanted to call him.

A few hours later Piper was in her apartment packing her bags to go home when her phone rang. Piper looked at the screen and it was Grace.

"Hey Grace. I can't really talk; I have to go home my..." Just then, Grace cut her off.

"I know Piper. I'm on my way now. I'm going to drive you home," Grace said, determined. "I will not take no for an answer. You can't drive like this, not that far anyway. I'll be there in five," Grace said as she hung up so Piper could not try to talk her out of it.

Grace pulled up to the front of Piper's apartment building not long after she hung up the phone. As she made her way inside, she ran into Piper in the hallway. Piper was placing her bags outside of her apartment door, and Grace could see Piper was a wreck. Her face was red and swollen, her makeup that she was sure she placed neatly on her face this morning, was now leaving streak marks down her cheeks. Just as Piper set her last bag in front of her door, Grace grabbed her and hugged her tight and close.

"Thank you for coming, Grace," Piper said as she released Grace from her embrace. "I was planning to drive, but you are right, there is no way I could drive like this. Not that far anyway," Piper said, making her way to her bathroom to wash her face and change her clothes for the long drive ahead of her.

"I know. Your brother called and told me what was going on with your mom. When I found out I packed a bag and jumped in my car. Matthew told me you could use your dad's old truck when you get there if you need it. So, I knew it would not be a problem if I drove you and left you there for a while."

An hour later the friends were in Grace's car making their way to see Lucy in the hospital. In the back seat sat three stuffed bags. Piper had no idea how long she would be with her mom for, so she was prepared for anything. As they drove the radio stayed off and Grace felt enough time had passed to talk to Piper about the past few weeks.

"Hey so, I'm sorry about the past few weeks. I know I have been MIA; I have been pouting about nonsense," Grace apologized.

"No Grace, I was the one who overstepped. I'm sorry. I feel even worse about Rachel," she said softly.

"Yeah, she was so mad. Have you talked at all since that day?" Grace asked.

"Not really. I tried to call her, see her, and I even showed up to her place," she paused, "nothing," Piper said as she looked out the window.

"Do you have any of the specific details about your mom?" Grace asked gently. "Any idea how she ended up in the hospital?" Grace asked as she looked over at Piper, who shook her head.

"Well," Grace said through a sigh, "Matthew said she was at work, and she began to throw up." Piper paused, and tears began to build up. "She had some headaches for the past few weeks, but she didn't think much of it. But when she started to throw up, her co-worker called an ambulance and that's all I really know right now," she said as she looked out of the car window. "Matthew may know more by now. We will see when we get to the hospital."

Just as they pulled into Ardentville, Piper's hometown, Piper's phone buzzed. As she looked down, she saw it was her brother Matthew. Matthew told her that their mom was asleep for the night and that he would meet her at the house and give her all the details of what was going on.

Piper's phone buzzed again. This time it was a call from Rand. After letting him know what was going on, Rand told Piper he would meet her in Ardentville in the morning.

Grace turned onto Pine Street, the street Piper and Matthew grew up on and Piper's stomach sank. As they passed by the neighbor's houses, neighbors were out raking leaves, turning them into piles and watching as little kids and dogs jumped into the piles. Others were on their lawns decorating for Halloween. Some were walking in pairs and others were trailing kids on bikes. As the sky grew a bit grayer, and the chill became a little heavier, the lights in the neighborhood began flicking on.

When they got closer to Piper's house, Piper felt sick. She knew when she got to her mom's house, it would be dark. Cold. Lonely. But to her surprise, as they pulled into the driveway, Matthew's BMW sitting next to Piper's dad's old green 1949 Chevy 3100 pick up, the tarp that had been covering it was still in place. Piper exhaled as Grace placed her hand on Piper's knee. Piper grabbed Grace's hand and she squeezed it, tight. Hearing the car in the driveway, Matthew made his way outside to greet Piper and Grace. Since Piper and Grace had known each other since middle school, Grace was extremely comfortable with Matthew and Piper took notice of the eyes they gave each other.

"Hey," Matthew said as the screen door closed behind him. Piper noticed how exhausted he looked. She was not sure if it was from the new baby or from the stress, he was feeling. Piper assumed it was probably both. As Matthew made his way toward Piper, she cried, and she fell into his arms.

Matthew, younger than Piper, but not by much, was a former NFL tight end whose career was cut short by a knee injury. His brown hair was cut short and neat. He was a bit taller than 6'4", so when he held her, she felt safe and protected. They embraced for a few minutes and then released her to grab her bags.

"Hey Grace," Matthew said to Grace with his hands full of Piper's bags and a head nod in her direction.

"Hey," Grace said as she grabbed her bag out of the back seat. Piper stood outside on the porch afraid to walk in. But as Matthew and Grace made their way in, Piper did too. An hour later, the three sat in the kitchen eating Chinese take-out and Matthew explained what was going on.

"The doctor said it's Glioblastoma, GBM, stage 2. It is the most common, but it's also the most aggressive kind of tumor. She's going to have surgery tomorrow morning. After that the doctor will know more," Matthew explained with a lump in his throat.

He placed his hand on Piper's knee just as his phone rang. Pulling it out of his pocket, he looked down and saw it was his wife. He answered as he stood brushing Piper's shoulder and went into the other room. Piper sat in her chair, across from the chair her mother always sat in, and felt as if she could not breathe. She could hear Matthew on the phone talking to Laura about the baby and filling her in on Mom's surgery tomorrow.

Grace got up, grabbed the bottle of unopened wine on the counter, grabbed glasses, opened the door leading to the patio outside and motioned for Piper to join her. Piper got up, gestured to Matthew they were going outside and met Grace on the patio. As Grace wrestled with the wine bottle, Matthew came out and grabbed the bottle from her and they started to laugh.

"Grace, you have never been good at this," he said as he poured wine into the three glasses.

After placing his wine on the outdoor side table, he grabbed a pile of wood and lit the fire pit. The night got older, the wine got lower, and the three laughed, talked, cried and ate more until the early hours of the next day slowly crept up on them.

"Rand will be here tomorrow," Piper said staring into the fire.

"So, tell me about him," Matthew suggested to get her mind off her mom.

"Well, oddly he's a neurosurgeon. He works out of Ardentville Hospital occasionally. We met at the hospital in Boston, sort of a fluke," Piper said with a smile. "As soon as he heard about mom, he changed his schedule to be here." She paused, "We have seen each other a few times, we have not taken it to the next level yet." She trailed off.

"Okay," Matthew paused, "but he sounds like a man who knows what is important to him." Matthew said, "I can't wait to meet him."

"You will tomorrow. Probably at the hospital. But

I'm not sure."

Piper's phone buzzed. Rachel's name popped up on the screen.

"I need to take this call," Piper said as she got up and walked back into the house.

"Hey Rachel."

"I heard about your mom. Are you okay? I can be there tomorrow if you need me to." Rachel's words spilled out like a tipped over glass of water.

"Thank you, Rachel," Piper's voice cracked. "I really needed to hear from you. I'm so sorry for overstepping."

"It's okay. Don't worry about it. We have bigger things to worry about right now," Rachel said gently. "I have an author reading this weekend, but I can cancel and be there for you?"

"It's okay. I know how important that reading is to you. I want you to go. Grace is here, Matthew is here, and Rand will be here tomorrow," Piper explained.

"Rand? Oooo. That's kind of nice huh?" she asked.

Piper could not help but smile, appreciating the distraction thinking of Rand showing up for her without asking him to. "Yeah, I think so too."

"How are things with you guys?" Rachel asked trying to distract her friend.

"So far good. Not a lot of progress, but I am hoping for more. Timing is off right now, but we will see."

"I get that. Just concentrate on you and your family and see how things unfold naturally," Rachel said.

The two hung up with promises of talking soon and keeping each other updated on each other's progress with the things that had been going on in their lives.

The Venue

"What do you think?" she asked him eagerly.

"I love it. I think it's beautiful. And covered in snow, if it snows, will be amazing and if not, it's still going to be beautiful," he said looking around. "A natural winter wonderland theme."

"A winery in the winter isn't the first choice of some brides, but we can do pretty much anything you want, except control the weather," Sally, the venue manager told them. "But it will be beautiful. What date are you looking at? Before we proceed, it would be a good idea to see if we have your date available."

"February 12th," they said in unison.

"That was cute," Sally said, "let me just check the books really quick." She opened her laptop and tapped a few times. "Okay we are good for February 12th. We have that open. What are we thinking? Would you like to move forward? I know you mentioned a winter wonderland theme, we can get that organized for you if you would like?" she asked.

"Can you give us a few minutes?" he asked.

"Absolutely," Sally said, "I'll go see if Ralphie, the head chef, can be ready to serve the tasting if you decide on River Valley Winery to host your wedding," and she disappeared behind two solid wood doors.

She turned to him with glee in her eyes. "What do you think? Do you love it? Should we do it?"

"Hell, yeah, we should do it. This place is incredible. But we can't let her know we are interested," he

explained.

"I love you," she said looking him and he turned and kissed her.

"Okay Ralphie says if you are a go, he is ready with the food tastings," Sally announced.

"We like it, but we are not so sure. Seeing it's in February, we may be able to get a better price elsewhere," he said.

"Oh, look at the time, we have that appointment at Pleasant Hill Winery in a bit, we should go babe," she said gathering her coat.

"Pleasant Hill huh," Sally said and paused. "How about if you seal the deal today, I give you an extra twenty-five percent off?" she offered.

"Twenty-five percent sounds good, but..." she trailed off.

"Twenty-five percent off is really good. Take it or leave it," Sally said, sensing what they were doing.

"We will take it," he said.

"Perfect, I'll grab Ralphie," Sally said, satisfied.

February 12
River Valley Winery

Sixteen

I Looked For You

Rachel stood in the half bath of Melody's, a first-time author with Cuppa Coffee Publishing. Melody lived in the top floor apartment just outside the city. Standing in front of the mirror, with her hands on the sink, Rachel checked out her makeup and hair. Her long, straight, black hair hung past her shoulders, and her eye makeup made her grey eyes pop even more than usual. As she stood in front of the mirror, she closed her eyes and inhaled deeply. She was excited about this night. It had been a long time coming. Since her recent promotion to editor in chief for Cuppa Coffee Publishing, Rachel was excited to attend her first Intimate Readings event.

Melody's book *Not Conforming* was the first book Rachel had published as editor-in-chief. Although Rachel didn't always attend readings of the authors she had seen through the process, Melody's was special. Rachel had worked so hard to get the job of editor-in-chief, so it meant a lot to her to accept the invitation Melody had extend to her.

Intimate Readings were fun. They were on a much smaller scale and authors would host them before their book was released to the public. Rachel washed her hands, adjusted her hair, and gave her outfit of tight black jeans and lucky deep-v olive green sweater one last look before leaving the bathroom to see who else had arrived.

She had hoped that Becky, her work nemesis, would skip the event tonight. Becky was always throwing digs at Rachel because Rachel had beat out Becky for the editor-in-chief job. Becky tried to make it known that she deserved the job by challenging the publisher Lydia's decision to go with Rachel and not her. Rachel was not sure if Becky would show up, but as she opened the door to the bathroom, she closed her eyes and hoped she would not see Becky.

Rachel put her phone away in the back pocket of her jeans and opened the door. On the other side of the door, Rachel made her way around the apartment. The top floor loft apartment, in the warehouse district, sat just a few miles outside of Boston. Formally a textile factory, the entire top floor of the building was renovated and turned into a spectacular dwelling. With exposed beams crisscrossing the high ceilings, exposed brick making up the majority of the walls and floor-to-ceiling windows making up the rest, Rachel could see touches of its former years peeking through. She took it all in, the grand fireplace with a roaring fire, hard wood flooring throughout. Looking towards the stairs, she could see the master bedroom. Rachel could not see how the room was set up, but she knew it was probably amazing.

Looking over at Melody, as she set up her book display and talked to a few friends by the large stone fireplace, Rachel wondered if this place was her style or if it had belonged to Charles first. Charles and Melody didn't really match as a couple, Rachel remembered thinking when she first met them a year ago in her office. Melody, a 27-year-old free spirit hippie type of woman with short brown hair and a slim figure, and Charles, an older man, maybe in his early 50s and a well-known architect, was shorter than Melody. But when they were near each other, the love poured out of them. They didn't look like a match, but they were for sure a match when it came to each other. Snapping out of her memory, Rachel noticed the double sliding doors leading to the balcony, and she made her way through them.

With the sun setting and the early October twilight air increasingly becoming colder, Rachel stood outside on the balcony and could see the lights of the city beginning to glow. As she stood outside, she crossed her arms for warmth. Just as Rachel was turning to walk back inside, she was face to face with Charles.

"Excuse me," Charles said holding a bundle of logs and making his way onto the balcony through the sliding doors, "I need to get the fire going. It's going to be a cold one tonight, but with this amazing view of the Boston skyline and the fact that we rarely use the balcony, it seemed like the logical idea," he said as he moved around the balcony placing the wood in the firepit and beginning to light it. Just as the fire caught, the string lights above their heads turned on and Rachel took it all in. Simply standing there near the building fire and under the lights, Rachel felt an odd comfort.

"No problem, Charles. I'm going to head back in and see if I can get a front row seat to the big show," Rachel said as she took one last look at everything the balcony had to offer including the view of the skyline during the evening hour.

"I think we have a few more people coming, so that may be a good idea. Here," Charles said as he poured white wine for Rachel and a glass for himself, "cheers to you Rachel. You were a massive help to my wife throughout this entire process," he said as their glasses clinked together, and each took a sip.

Rachel kept Charles company for a few more minutes and as he continued to get the fire going to a small roar, Rachel wondered if Becky would be one of those people they may be expecting. The two made small talk around the glowing fire about the book and the process of how it all works. Rachel told Charles she admired Melody for being brave enough to share her story of placing her child up for adoption while she was still in high school. She knew it wasn't an easy story to write and although Rachel had never been through it, Melody's writing took her through her entire journey and while reading. Rachel felt as if she was the one giving up the baby. As Charles got the fire going to where he was happy with it, he refilled both of their glasses and Rachel made her way inside.

Holding her wine glass in one hand, and slightly closing the slider door with the other, Rachel heard the doorbell ring. Thoughts of Becky with her loud blond hair and unnecessary eye makeup filled Rachel's mind. The last person she wanted to see walk through that door was Becky, until the door opened.

Standing in the doorway, slightly behind but taller than a young blonde woman was a face she instantly recognized. Dark skin, full head of freshly cut hair, dark eyes, and a perfectly manicured beard resting on his face. With his full lips and rounded symmetrical nose sitting just above his mouth, Rachel's heart dropped into her stomach. Shock took over her entire body while heat rushing through her blood reminded her to breathe. As they made their way into the loft apartment, the blonde woman recognized someone she knew, and she headed toward them. Rachel, still in shock, made clear eye contact with the man that she had known for years and as he began to recognize her, Rachel dropped her wine glass, sending pieces of shattered glass flying everywhere.

"Rachel?" He asked with a confused look on his face.

Rachel, still in slight shock, looked at him. She knew this day would eventually arrive. Under her breath, she said, "Marcus."

As one of the servers cleaned up the wine and the shards of glass, Marcus slowly made his way towards Rachel and Charles pulled her aside to see if she was okay.

"Everything okay Rachel?" Charles asked with concern. "Do you know him? Is there a problem?" he continued to ask to make sure she was okay.

"I'm okay, Charles. I do know him," she said looking at him from across the room. His eyes were on her, and she could see the anticipation crawling out of his body as he waited to talk to her. "He is someone from my past and I was just shocked to see him here tonight. I wasn't expecting this."

"Ahh. okay. Well, if you need some time to talk, please take it. Melody will understand," he said as he gestured with his hand over to Marcus to come over to where they were standing.

"Thanks Charles, I have no idea how this will go. I messed up big time and I owe him an explanation," she said shamefully as Marcus walked toward them.

Charles patted Marcus on the shoulder, head nodded toward Rachel and walked away to join the reading that was just beginning.

"Rachel," Marcus said, "what happened to you? I looked for you everywhere," he said sounding both panicked and relieved.

Rachel, grabbing his arm, pulled him toward the direction of the balcony. "Let's talk out here," Rachel said as she slid the double doors open and the air stung them both.

On the balcony they could see the lights of the city were now bright and glowing, and the fire Charles had built was now full and keeping the seating area around it warm. Rachel and Marcus took a seat on the soft outdoor sofa closest to the fire. With the two sitting close, almost touching, Marcus eagerly opened the conversation.

The Wedding Dress

There were endless attempts of putting on and taking off dresses, discovering a lot of dresses look better on a hanger. Even while exhausted and on the verge of giving up, her friends made everything better. With each fail she walked out in, the friends laughed, held out signs with numbers on them and of course toasted each and every one regardless of whether it was loved, hated or next'd. Eventually, the group went rogue and picked out what they wanted her to try on.

When she first saw the dress she was now wearing, she rolled her eyes and tried it on to simply satisfy her friends. She figured if she tried on the dresses they suggested, she could get back to finding the perfect ball gown. But to her shock, the instant the dress began to cover her body from the ankles up, she felt it. She felt the feeling every bride has while searching for her wedding dress. When the V-neck, cold shoulder spaghetti strap dress was zipped all the way up, she covered her mouth with both hands and tears filled her eyes. Even before stepping outside of the dressing room, she knew this was the one.

After trying on dress after dress after dress, she came out with a smile on her face and tears in her eyes.

"I think this is the one guys," she said as she stepped on to the platform.

She stood in front of the mirror and looked herself up and down. A slight twirl to the left and then one to the right. In the mirror before her, she could see

134 | KELLY SMITH

her friends sitting on the white wrap around couch holding their champagne glasses and looking absolutely stunned. No one said a word. They couldn't.

The bridal assistant walked over, placed a long veil on her head and stood back.

"What do you think of this one?" the assistant asked.

She stood in disbelief, and her friends huddled around her.

"Are you going to say yes to the dress?" the assistant asked.

In the floor-length gown, covered in lace and tulle, she said yes to the dress.

Seventeen

Letting Him Go

Sydney began her day with a group text from Piper updating everyone on her mom's progress. This morning's update was that she was still in the hospital and heading into surgery soon. With Andrew out of town and some of her friends in Ardentville, Sydney continued to train for her race that was fast approaching. When she tried to be there for Piper, she was turned down. Piper told her she had enough support with her especially since Rand was there, but she still wanted to try to do their book club meeting, if possible. Everyone agreed and would make the time if Piper could. They wanted to be as supportive as they could for Piper and her family.

Sydney was leaving the gym; her phone rang, and Andrew's name flashed across her screen. With a smile on her face, she answered and made her way to her car. Andrew had been traveling to film his show and he was headed back to Boston, and he had news to share with Sydney.

When they hung up Sydney was eager to see him again later that night. Their relationship was going well. Although he was gone a lot, and Sydney was busy, they made the best of the time they spent together. As she drove back to her apartment, she thought back to the day they made their relationship official.

They were in her bakery, and he was showing her a technique she was struggling with. She looked at him in his apron and marveled at his biceps wrapped in a tight T-shirt. For a minute she could not believe Andrew Casper was in her bakery, but then her heart melted, and she realized he was not Andrew Casper to her, he was Andrew, the man who had a rough childhood, allergies, and liked to be babied when he was sick. As she looked at him, she could see herself loving him long term and that scared her. She looked away and he asked if she was okay.

"Yeah, I'm good. I'm just trying to get this to look like yours," she said comparing both cupcakes.

"Syd," Andrew said looking at her.

"Yes," she replied without making eye contact.

He placed his cupcake on the table in front of him, and he took hers from her hand. He gently grabbed her hand and led her to the booth that sat in front of the picture window of The Lemon Bar.

"I have been having so much fun with you Syd. I think you're absolutely incredible and I have no idea why it was me at that elevator the day we met. I want to be with you, just you, and I want you to be with just me. What do you say?" he asked with his eyes big and his heart hopeful. "Do you want to be my girlfriend?"

Sydney paused. All the feelings running though her body. She wanted to be with Andrew but being with Andrew meant letting Daniel go and she was not sure if she was ready to do that just yet. Making it official was the first step to fully moving on.

"A few Christmases ago," Sydney began, "I spent the

holiday with Piper and her family. As we drove back to the city, a song came on and it brought up memories of Daniel. She could tell I was upset and pulled out of me what was upsetting me. As we sat in her car outside of my building, I told her how I was feeling, and I admitted that I was not sure I could ever love again. I am afraid to try. I'm afraid to try because what if I do find someone? I know he would want me to be happy, but I'm afraid of forgetting him. If someone else touches me, his touch will be gone. If someone kisses me, his kisses will be gone. I have no idea if I will ever be ready to let him go in that way," Sydney paused and looked at Andrew. His eyes still big and hopeful.

"How did she respond?" Andrew asked.

"She said that he will never be gone. Ever. He will always be in my heart and believe it or not I have room for someone else in there, but not until I'm ready," she said, looking in Andrew's hopeful eyes. She imagined what life would be without him and when she pictured herself not having him by her side, she felt sick. She knew it was time and she knew she wanted it to be Andrew.

"Yes. I will be your girlfriend," she said. She got up, sat next to him, and kissed him. "You better not be using me for my bakery," she said laughing.

"Oh man, you caught me."

Sydney snapped out of her memory as she got out of her car and went into her apartment. Later that night, Andrew picked up Sydney from her apartment and said he had a surprise for her. He refused to tell her where they were going. They drove and chatted and caught up on their busy lives between seeing each other until Andrew pulled up in front of a building Sydney didn't recognize. As she got out of the car, she questioned what was going on. Andrew grabbed her hand and led her inside. They stepped onto the elevator and went to the top floor.

"Andrew?' Sydney questioned, "what are we doing here?" she asked.

"You will see," he said with a smile on his face.

As they stepped off the elevator, they were in an apartment and a man was waiting to greet them as they stepped inside.

"Tim!" Andrew said, shaking the man's hand.

"Great to see you, Andrew! And this must be Sydney," Tim said as he held his hand out for Sydney to shake, and she did.

Sydney clung closer to Andrew, still confused but beginning to understand what may be going on.

Tim guided them around the apartment. A spacious one with two bedrooms, two full bathrooms, hardwood floor throughout, and of course floor to ceiling windows that opened to a wraparound balcony. The views off the master and living room were of the city and the city skyline, while the views from the second bedroom and the master chef kitchen offered views of the river and surrounding parks.

"Andrew! This place is gorgeous," she said as she held his hand and let him lead her for a tour also guided by his real-estate agent.

"And if you look out of the French doors leading to the balcony off the master, you may just be able to see your favorite hot spots from the comfort of your own home," Tim, Andrew's agent said as he opened the doors and began to walk outside. "Can you imagine being anywhere but here on New Year's Eve? The fireworks display the city puts on is magnificent. You two could make some beautiful memories here," he said and even through Andrew's dark skin, Sydney could see him blushing and he held her hand tighter.

As they made their way through the rest of the penthouse, Tim explained that there was a doorman 24/7. A special key was needed to access the private elevator that opened directly to the living room and as a bonus, the penthouse came with a weekly cleaning service. The rest of the penthouse was amazing. The top-of-the-line kitchen appliances, the touchless sinks and the LED rectangular rainfall shower head was something that the two had both never heard of but also now they didn't want to live without. This penthouse was the one Andrew really loved. He had looked at one or two others, but this one struck a chord with him, so it meant something for him to get Sydney's approval. He could also see them building a life together there over time.

After leaving the building, Andrew and Sydney went to grab a drink and talk about the penthouse. By the time the day had turned to night, drinks were drunk, and appetizers turned into dinner and then dessert, it was decided. Andrew was going to move forward with the purchase of the penthouse and the fancy color changing shower head and officially move to Boston. Officially move closer to Sydney.

The next day as Andrew was filing paperwork and making his move official, Sydney was in the bakery with an apron wrapped around her waist. She listened to music and let her mind wonder just a bit, as she was lost in thought, she had an idea. The thought about the name of her bakery, "The Lemon Bar" and she looked around the bakery. She grabbed her phone and called Andrew.

"Hey," he answered.

"Hi, how's the paperwork coming along?" She asked.

"I just finished. You okay?" he asked.

"Yeah, I have an idea actually, any chance you can stop by the bakery?"

"On my way!" he said, and they disconnected the call.

As they stood in the bakery both looking around and thinking along the same lines, Andrew said, "You know what Syd, I think this can work,"

"You think so? You think I could turn the bakery in to an evening lounge that serves baked goods and coffee during the day and baked goods and cocktails in the evening?"

"I really do. I think so because people like to eat when they drink. Yeah, they like greasy food, but cupcakes, cookies and pastries are not a bad option," he said standing close to her.

"I think I'm going to look into it," she said smiling.

"I love this idea Syd, and I will help in any way you need me to," he said kissing her forehead.

"Thank you," she said.

"Okay I need to get going. I have a few more things on my to do list for today. I will see you tonight," he said as he headed out the door.

After Andrew left, she took in her new idea. And she imagined how her life would be different if Daniel never died. At times she imagined him there in the city and living in her new apartment. But she was thinking of Daniel less and less. He was still there with her in her heart and that would never change, but she was feeling more and more comfortable with Andrew and the thought of being with him was not so scary anymore. As she stood in her bakery, she thought back to the first time she ever saw Andrew.

She was at Daniel's house, sitting on the couch waiting for him to pour her a glass of the wine she had brought over. Daniel was due to be back at the station the next day, and she always made it a point to spend the night before he left for his 48-hour shift with him. As they got comfy on the couch and just seconds before her favorite baking live TV show began, an advertisement came blaring across the screen announcing a new bakeoff challenge show. Andrew, a baker the producers discovered in a small restaurant in California, would be the judge.

As she watched the commercial and sipped her wine, she noticed how attractive Andrew was and she made a note to watch the show—mainly because of the premise, but seeing him could be a bonus.

Over time, Andrew Casper became a household name. He was never in the media in a negative light. He was one of these guys that taught baking lessons at elementary schools, volunteered his time, and made fun surprise appearances to his fans.

Meeting him was never an idea that came across Sydney's mind, and now he was in her life, fully in her life and in living color. She wondered how life would be after Andrew moved to Boston. Sydney was a little nervous about losing some of her freedom with him living there full time. She was, in a way, set in her ways. She had the freedom to go out after work, see friends for their rituals, and come and go as she pleased. She wanted to be with Andrew, but she didn't want to lose herself or her friends for a relationship. How much of that would change when Andrew was near her full time?

Save the date

"Are you ready?" she asked him as she stood in the doorway of the kitchen.

"Yeah, just give me a few," he said.

"Okay but I don't want to wait much longer. I'm meeting with the girls to discuss bridesmaid dress shopping this afternoon," she reminded him.

"Why do I need to go with you for this? I mean it's a piece of paper, can't you just go? You know what I like," he said, annoyed.

"Are you serious? We are supposed to be planning this wedding together," she complained.

"We are, but every inch needs to be together?" he questioned.

"Okay fine, I'll just go," she said as she grabbed her handbag and headed towards the garage door.

"Wait," he called out, "I'll go with you."

"I don't want your pity time," she said as she reached for the door handle.

He grabbed her, pulled her in close for a hug. As she laid her head on his chest, she began to cry.

"What's wrong?" he asked, pushing her out so he could look at her.

"I'm just stressed. This a lot of work and I want to have this experience with you," she paused. "I have expectations and they include you. Maybe I should let those go?"

"I understand," he said wiping her tears. "I'll be honest, a lot of this stuff is boring to me. I don't understand it and I have no idea what the difference between off white, eggshell, and bear white is. I don't want to be unhelpful to you. But," he pushed her hair behind her ear and kissed her cheek, "I do love seeing you happy and I love the time we spend together."

She smiled up at him and wiped her face, "You don't know the difference between those colors?" she asked. "Maybe I should go alone." They both laughed.

"Come on, let's go pick out some boring weird color that looks like white," he opened the garage door, and she slipped through.

Weeks later they stood in the post office about to drop 150 save-the-dates in the outgoing mailbox.

"I have never been more ready for anything in my life," he said as he smiled at her and opened the mail-box.

In her hands she held the stack of envelopes all tied together with twine. She looked at him and her face lit up.

"I am so happy right now. I simply can't wait to marry you," she said.

"Let's do it," he said.

She untied the twine wrapped around the enve-lopes, kissed him on the lips and dropped them in.

"We did it!" she squealed as he grabbed her hand and walked out of the post office.

Eighteen
The Doctor Is In

As the sun began to peek through the purple curtains in her childhood bedroom, Piper's head hurt. The sun was bright and intrusive. For a minute Piper forgot why she was there and then suddenly it all came rushing back to her. She laid in her bed on her back silently. She didn't look at her phone. She didn't get up. She just took in the meaning of the day and inhaled without making a sound.

Outside of her bedroom door she could hear Grace and Matthew in the kitchen and moments later her room and nostrils were full of the smell of coffee. She rolled over, grabbed her phone, and made her way to the kitchen. When she got into the kitchen, she saw Laura holding Chase, her nephew, on FaceTime with Grace and Matthew. She popped her head in between the two to say hi as she grabbed a mug from the cabinet.

After the call ended and the coffee was consumed, they got ready and headed to the hospital. They drove together in Matthew's car, Grace in the front seat and Piper in the back. From the backseat Piper felt she could hide away from everything. As they made their way to the hospital, Piper saw her little town pass by her in a flash.

Although she came home from the city often, Piper was seeing her town with different eyes, and she felt as if she was seeing it for the first time. The shops were getting ready for the annual Halloween Carnival the town hosted for the high school football team each year. The parade, the pageant, and then the carnival right after was something the town looked forward to each October. The shops and restaurants were decorated as either a haunted house for the teenagers or a pumpkin patch for the kids. Piper always had fun, but never understood why the girls wanted to be crowned Miss Ghoul. She never participated, but she assured herself that if she had, she would have won, easy.

When they passed the high school, Piper fell into a memory of Blake. Blake Powell was Piper's high school sweetheart and the one she thought she was going to marry. As the image of him the last time she saw him slipped into her mind, she shook herself out of it and realized they were at the hospital. Crawling out of the car, Piper's mind and body was feeling so much. Sadness, confusion, and fear. They made their way to the entrance, elevator, until eventually they walked through the doors of Piper's mother's hospital room.

Her mother was in her bed, eyes closed, and she looked pale. Emotions built up in Piper's stomach and eventually fell out of her eyes. As one tear chased another, her mother opened her eyes and saw her family by her bedside.

"Piper?" her mother said, looking in her direction and seemingly shocked to see her there, "you didn't have to come all this way just for me," she said reaching out her hand to grab Piper's hand.

"Of course, I didn't have to Mom, I wanted to. This is a big deal," she said now sitting in a nearby chair holding both of her mother's hands. Piper noticed her hair was grayer, her hands were frailer, and her eyes, although they looked the same, they now held something different in them.

Piper could not help but imagine a younger, healthier version of her mom. The version of her mom that took her shopping for her prom dress. The version that cheered her on during her dance performances. The version that helped her pick out and decorate her dorm room. The version of her who filled the entire room with happiness when she laughed. The version of her that hugged so well and made breakfast like no one else. And of course, the version that held her as she told her about the breakup with Blake.

And then there was the other side of her mom, the broken side. She envisioned her mom after her dad died. And the version that picked up the pieces and held them together in front of everyone, but Piper knew behind closed doors her mother was falling apart. But right here and now, Piper was meeting a version of her mother she didn't like and didn't want to know. While sitting next to her, the doctor walked in.

"Good morning, Lucy," Dr. Baker said as he made his way into the room and pulled a chair up so he could sit. "How are you feeling today?" he asked as he nodded to everyone in the room. "Looks like we have a full house this morning."

"Good morning, Doctor," Lucy struggled the words out, "yes, my son Matthew, you met him yesterday. My daughter Piper and her best friend Grace. They came from the city to be with me," she said as she smiled at Grace.

"I am glad you have a great support system," Dr. Baker said matter of factly. "Okay, today's surgery,"

Dr. Baker began. They heard what the procedure was, removing the tumor, as much as they could get. He was not sure what he was going to find exactly but would know more once inside. He went on to explain the risks, asked if anyone had any questions, and just as he was wrapping up, a familiar face walked in. Rand.

"Ah, here he is, this is Dr. Rand Melvin," Dr. Baker announced, "I heard he was here because of the connection he has with Piper," he said as he looked at Piper with a smile. "He's going to be in with me, per his request. I will be the one to operate, but I wanted to keep you updated on what will be going on in the surgical room," he trailed off.

As the nursing staff prepped Lucy to head to the OR, Rand pulled Piper aside.

"Are you okay? I'm sorry you are just seeing me now; I got in early this morning and had a few patients to catch up with. But I wanted to check on you," he explained.

"It's really good to see you," she said. "I didn't know you would be in with her, that makes me feel better."

"I will only be observing for a bit, then I'll come out and sit with you for a bit," he kissed her forehead and made his way to the OR.

"If you want to follow me," a nurse said, "I'll take you to the waiting room. The cafeteria is on the third floor. The food isn't amazing, but it will keep you from going hungry. Coffee is in the waiting room, have as much as you like."

As the hours began to pass, Grace's phone rang. She had to get home for work, "I'm sorry Piper, I have to go, but I can come back in a few days," Grace said with sadness on her face. "Will you be okay?" she asked.

Piper got up and hugged her friend. "Thank you,"

she whispered to Grace. "I will be fine. I will call you and keep you updated with the progress."

"I'll be back in a bit, and I'll bring some food, some real food," Matthew said as he hugged his sister. "I need to stop by the house to check on Laura and Chase, but I won't be gone long. Let me know as soon as you hear anything," Matthew said as he grabbed his coat and placed his hand on the small of Grace's back. Piper thought that was curious and made a mental note to ask Matthew about that later.

A few minutes after Matthew and Grace left, Rand walked into the waiting area.

"Hey. How are you holding up?" he asked, handing her a fresh cup of coffee.

"I'm as good as I can be under the circumstances," she said, taking the cup from him.

He sat in the chair next her and crossed his legs, "Everything is going well so far," he said. "I don't have much to update you on."

"I figured," she said blankly.

The two sat close and talked for a few minutes. When Rand's phone buzzed, he got up and said he had to make a few calls but would check on her soon. Piper got up and hugged Rand. This hug was different. It was full on and tight. Piper leaned her head on Rand's chest, and he held her until she released him.

Just as she was picking up her phone to call Matthew, he walked through the door holding bags of fast food in one hand and drinks in the other. "Hey Piper, I dropped Grace off, saw the family and got some food. Sorry it took so long," he said, emptying his hands and placing the bags and drinks on the table in front of Piper.

"No, it's fine. Thanks for taking Grace back to the

house. While you were gone Rand came in. He said he didn't have an update as of yet," she said, taking bites of food between breaths.

Matthew dropped his food back onto the table, threw his head into his large hands and cried. Piper got up and made her way to her younger brother and helped him. He turned into her shoulder, grabbed her, and sobbed. Through his tears he told Piper how scared he was of losing their mom. He told how alone he felt after he got the call that she was hurt at work. He told Piper how hard it had been pretending he was strong. Piper held her brother until his tears were empty, until he had none left. He sat up, lifting his head from her shoulder, and told her he loved her. He extended his arm, pulling her into his chest, and kissed the top of her forehead.

Nineteen
Pitman's Park

Before Grace knew it, she was on the road headed back to the city from Ardentville. As she drove, she realized she had not heard much from Dax. It bothered her because he knew where she was and the fact that he didn't check in at all made her start to really consider that maybe something was up with him, but could it be he was with someone else altogether? As Grace drove home, she sent Daxton a text. She felt as if she needed to vent about what was going on with Daxton, so she called Sydney.

"Hey everything okay?" answered Sydney.

"Yeah, everything is okay as far as I know. Lucy was in surgery when I left. I had to go back to work, but Piper said she would update us as soon as she knows anything. Do you have a few?" Grace asked solemnly.

"Yeah Grace, what's up? You okay? Is it Daxton?" Sydney asked.

"I have been thinking about what Piper said about Daxton. Do you think he could be engaged? After we met and had that conversation, I was so angry. But after I calmed down, I realized Piper isn't going to say something to hurt me just because. I know it wasn't easy for her or for you guys to point things out me, so now I am just confused. Have I just been making excuses for him?" she asked.

"Nowadays Grace, you just don't know. I think this is something you have to give some thought and maybe ask him about it? Would you be willing to do that?" she asked.

Sydney did somewhat believe Daxton very well may be engaged or was at least seeing someone else. She knew though, if she pushed the issue, she would also be pushing away her friend. All of Grace's friends knew she was adamant about figuring things out on her own and their responsibility was to be there for her when she's figured it all out.

"Yeah, you're right. I just have to ask. I don't think he's engaged, that's ridiculous. But I can bring it up at the right time. But it's a risk, if he's not engaged, and truly busy, then he can walk away because of my accusations, but again, even if he is engaged, he's not going to admit it to me." She paused trying to solve all of her problems in that moment.

"It's okay Grace," Sydney said, "It's okay to not know everything, and it's okay to wonder what's going on. He has not been a stand-up guy with you, so maybe the question you should be asking is why you want a guy like him in the first place. Engaged or not, I don't think he's good for you," Sydney bravely said.

"Well, I never thought of it that way," Grace admitted, "but I still want to know what his deal is."

"I get that. You know we will be here for you if or when you need us. We love you and we will support as much as we can," Sydney said.

As Grace was disconnecting the call with Sydney, her phone buzzed. It was Daxton.

They had spent the cold, October night strolling around Pitman's Park while sipping hot cider and looking at Halloween decorations, hand in hand. From one spooky display to the next, they had laughed and talked and enjoyed their surroundings. Grace was taking it all in as she stood by a larger-than-life Jack-o-lantern, all lit up, while she waited for Daxton to come back from the bathroom inside Pittman's Park. She watched Daxton make his way back to her, noticing him shut off his phone as soon as they made eye contact. When he put his phone into his jacket pocket, Grace felt all warm inside. She was thrilled he wanted to spend time with just her, no phone to distract them. When he had called the other day, while Grace was leaving Ardentville, to invite her out for that night, she found out his mom had been sick, and that's why he was MIA, and all of her worries about him faded away. For the next few hours, they made their way around the park. Scents of fried dough filled the air, people buzzed by with strollers, the flashing of camera lights went off around them, and they huddled together to keep warm. Grace was content.

When they made their way back to his car, Grace thought maybe now would be a good time to have a conversation with Daxton.

"Dax," she said as he shut the car door behind him and was turning on the heat in the car. "I wanted to talk to you about something." Daxton looked up at her with concern now splashed across his face.

"Is it something that can wait? Maybe until we are settled back at your place?" he asked, hoping it wasn't anything serious.

"Sure," she responded with a smile on her face as she took his hand in hers and began to warm it up for him.

As they drove, not much was said. It was an awkward silence. Grace felt weird, but in her head, she was going over the things she wanted to ask. First, she thought to herself, I will let him know that I have really enjoyed the time I have been spending with him. Then, her thoughts continued, I will say, "Since it's been a few months, where do you see this going?" Her mouth was suddenly dry and her stomach in knots as she saw her apartment building. She knew after they got inside, she wouldn't be brave enough to bring this up until they opened a bottle of wine and she had her first glass.

"Grace, I can't come up tonight," Daxton stated. "I have an early morning meeting to get to and I'll be busy for the rest of this week. So, I am not sure when I will see you again. But I promise this will slow down soon."

"Oh," she said with disappointment as she felt the knots in her stomach turn to bricks. "Well, I wanted to talk to you about something important to me, do you have a few minutes now?" she asked.

"I really wish I did, but I don't. I really have to get going. But I will text you later, Okay?" his puppy dog eyes looked directly at her.

Although disappointed, she was also slightly relieved. She was not sure she was ready to have that conversation just yet, so she took it as a sign to wait a bit longer.

"Okay, I understand," she said as her stomach dropped. She didn't have a good feeling about this, about him saying he didn't want to go upstairs and saying he was going to be busy for an undetermined amount of time. She started to think that maybe Piper was right.

A few minutes after entering her apartment, she had taken off her coat, grabbed a glass of wine, pulled out her secret stash of peanut M&Ms she ate when she was stressed, and called Rachel.

Rachel heard her phone buzz. She checked to see if it

was Piper with any update. When she saw it was Grace, she put her phone back on the table in front of her.

"I don't understand what happened to you?" Marcus began. "One day you were in my apartment, and the next day you were gone. Were things really that bad that you didn't want to talk to me anymore? Do you have any idea how much I looked for you? The last night I saw you, you threw a paper at me, I kept it. And after a few days when I didn't hear from you and after I tried to call you and your number was changed, I got worried. I called the publishing house on that offer letter," he said as he made direct eye contact with her.

"You did what?" Rachel asked horrified. Marcus, placing his hand on her leg, continued.

"I had no idea where you were. I thought this was just another fight. Just another argument. I figured after a few days of cooling off, you would call me, but when I didn't hear from you, I panicked. So yes, I called. And they told me you didn't take the job. When I asked for any more information, they said they couldn't help me. I called your parents, friends and looked all over the internet and could not find you anywhere. No one would help me. Your dad told me you were fine and when you were ready you would reach out. But Rachel, it's been twelve months! Twelve months, Rachel. Are you still not ready to talk to me?" he asked as he moved his hand from her leg.

Rachel, hearing everything Marcus said, looked off toward the lights of the city. She inhaled, closed her eyes, and tried to warm her hands by holding them to the fire. Turning and looking at Marcus, Rachel knew she had to talk to him. She had to tell him why she left and basically disappeared.

She looked into his dark brown eyes, the eyes she

had looked into the first day they met. The dark brown eyes she looked into as they made love for the first time. The dark brown eyes that she wiped tears from after they watched a war movie. The day she had met him, she had no idea how much he was going to mean to her. As their relationship grew, they became so close. She didn't expect things to end the way did, and it hurt so much.

Snapping out of her memories of meeting the now near stranger sitting close to her, Rachel inhaled slightly, allowing the cold air to enter her body, and she adjusted herself away from the fire and towards Marcus. Looking at him now, sitting near her, she allowed the feelings she had been pushing down for the past year to overcome her. She had missed him every day since she walked away from him. She thought of him so much and so many times she wanted to call him or go see him. But she also knew she deserved better in not only a relationship but in life as well. Just because she loved him more than she had ever loved anyone, did not mean she had to suffer not so silently or live uncomfortably because of love. She had to love herself more than she loved anyone and that meant she had to protect herself.

Seeing the pain in his eyes still alive made her feel guilty. Up until this point she didn't feel bad about how she left. She didn't feel bad that she changed her number, and she didn't feel bad that she removed herself entirely from social media. But now guilt was enveloping her, and she hated seeing how much he was hurting. It was in his eyes, in his words, and all over his face. In this moment Rachel was battling both guilt and relief seeing him again.

"I'm sorry, Marcus," Rachel said looking at him and grabbing his hand at the same time. "I am so sorry.

What I did was wrong, and I should not have left you in that way. You deserved better than that," she admitted as she squeezed and held his hand, and he squeezed back.

Rachel was surprised at how calm he seemed as they sat together. The Marcus she knew would have been irritated and it would have been apparent. The Marcus she knew was selfish and mostly concerned with his side of things. Rarely did he apologize, admit he was wrong or even seem to care if Rachel's feelings were hurt. But this Marcus sitting close to her, with his hand in hers, seemed calmer, even understanding. His aura was different.

She remembered, years ago, Marcus being short with her when she would ask a question or if she was standing in the kitchen too close to him. She had no idea if how he was presenting now, under a cold star filled night sky, was the true him or just an act. Feeling as if she wanted to test the waters, she continued her apology.

"When I left," she said still holding his hand and with her voice shaking from uncertainty, she continued, "I was angry. Hurt. Confused. Honestly, I was all of it. I was every emotion I felt," she paused now, looking away from him, "that day, the last day I saw you, you were so uninterested in me, in my accomplishments. I had worked so hard to get that position and I was excited to tell you about it. To share my news with you and you just...you just wrote me off. That day was the last straw for me. For such a long time I tried to get your attention. Either you were working or wrapped up in your friends. A few months into dating you, I began to notice it. Your nights got longer; dates were cancelled, but the nights out with your friends remained. It bothered me but I kept an open mind. I knew your job was stressful and I was happy you got to release some energy. Looking back, I should have said something to you or just walked away, but I thought things would get better on their own, and they did on and off. I was confused because you seemed to want me around but were afraid to commit. I could not tell if you wanted me or if I was just background noise to you," she paused for a beat as tears began to build up behind her eyes. She blinked and they began to fall down her cheek.

Marcus let go of her hand and wiped away her tears. He inched closer to her and didn't say a word. He let her be still and waited for her to continue. "It was almost two years of dating, Marcus," she said as she turned to look at him, "two years and we were still dating or talking or whatever. I was frustrated because I wanted you, I wanted to be with you. And you had no idea if you wanted me or not. I was feeling unwanted, uncared for and ignored. The times I tried to leave, end things, you would not let me. Again, it seemed as if you wanted me but only for yourself. You didn't want to let me go because you didn't want anyone else to have me, but you didn't want me either. So... I left," she said, now becoming more and more hurt with the memories flooding back to her mind. "I left in the way I did because I knew you would not just let me go and I needed to get on with my life. I wanted more." She covered her face with her hands and let herself cry.

Sitting outside in the cold, next to the man she left over a year ago, she was hurt and angry. Blood rushed warmly throughout her body, and she didn't know if she wanted to hug him or knock his block off, but she did know that while the way she left wasn't right, it was necessary.

Beginning to calm down and as her tears dried, she told Marcus about leaving Lakeshore, the call from Cuppa Coffee and her decision to move to Boston and not California. "It was a quick decision. One I made because I knew I would miss my family and I wanted to be close just in case but mostly because it was a better position with high pay. I thought about you when I got the call. I wanted to call you and tell you all about it, but then I remembered the way you ignored me and the case you had been preparing for that monopolized most of your time at that point. So, I called my dad, and he helped me make the decision to take the job with Cuppa Coffee. It was that night," she continued as she sipped her wine, "that I moved into the most beautiful apartment I had ever seen up until that point. I met with Thomas, the building manager, who met me at the door and helped me bring my bags up as he gave me a tour of the building. After signing the contracts and having a video meeting with Lydia, for a semi on-boarding letting me know I would start work on that Monday, I sat on the couch in a brand-new place, looking out of the window seeing the busy city below me and I cried. I cried so hard. I was mad and confused, but mostly I was hurt. I wondered if you had noticed I had left yet. I missed you so much my stomach was turning," she said remembering how she felt that night. "I knew I had to either call you or begin to let you go. I made the decision to let you go because I felt if I called you, you would convince me that you would change things like you said you would before, and I would believe you again. I didn't trust myself around you. I had hope and hope had let me down before, so I made this decision," Taking a hefty swig of her wine, she looked at Marcus and could tell hearing all of this stung. But she also knew she had to get it out before he tried to take over the conversation and shut it down like he had done so often while they were together. She was a bit surprised he had not done so yet. "I know it may not have been the best decision for me to make, but I felt it was the best choice for me at that time."

As Marcus sat close to Rachel, he listened. He let her say what she needed to say. Rachel told him how she eventually made enough money with her promotions to buy the apartment right above the company's apartment. She spoke of getting lost in the city, mistakenly getting on one transportation shuttle when she needed to get on a different one, making her late for her first day and solidifying the nickname Wrong Bus Rachel, which was shortened over the years to just Wrong Bus, something she hated but learned to accept. She never took the bus again.

"This past year has been difficult, to say the least. At first, I was able to get lost in work. I worked a bunch, and it paid off rather quickly. I work for a company that lets me be creative and for that I'm grateful. They held parties and events, so socially I was busy as well. But most of the time I was faking it. Don't get me wrong, I was happy to be there and meeting new people, but I was still sad and had no idea how to heal from walking away from you. I reminded myself that you were non-committal, emotionally unavailable, and you placed your career ahead of this relationship. At one point, I cut strips of paper and on each one I wrote reasons why I should not reach out to you and placed them in a jar. Each time I wanted to call you, I pulled one out and it kept me from contacting you."

"After meeting my friends, they set me up on dates and I went. I even had fun. I was starting to let myself have fun. Piper is the head of the marketing for TOGETHER. She had an event and invited all of us to attend. That night, I met someone, Jared. He is an investment banker but has a passion for high-risk fun," she said as she thought of zip-lining with him and how she screamed the entire way across, and Jared thought it was insane how much she was screaming. "He was great. Handsome, funny, successful. We went out a few times. He treated me so well. I told him about you a bit. On one of our dates, he kissed me. It was actually nice and the first kiss I had since I left you. But after being on the couch with him and him trying to take things further, I opened up and told him I wasn't ready just yet."

As she continued to speak, Marcus, clearly uncomfortable with the direction the conversation was headed, squeezed her leg, and looked away. "But I wasn't ready. I wasn't ready to get into a relationship or even date someone consistently. I was not single; I was broken, and I had nothing to offer anyone at that point. So, I let him go. He understood, and still keeps in touch because he knows someday, I will be ready. And he's right. I will be. I am just about there, but not with him," she finished explaining and let out a sigh of relief.

Just as Rachel reached for her now-empty wine glass, Charles made an appearance on the balcony. He poured wine into their glasses and added logs to the steady fire. Charles could feel the tension in the air and left as soon as his duties were done.

The Bridesmaid Dresses

They walked into the bridal store and could not help but squeal. They were greeted by Judy, the bridal shop associate.

"Hey girls! We have been expecting you," she said. "We have picked out a great selection for you all, follow me back and I can you guys started on a few of these gowns," she said and the girls followed her.

As they all settled on the comfy oversized couch, had their glasses filled with champagne, and snacked on the fruit tray in front of them, Judy asked what the main thing was they wanted in their bridesmaid dress. In unison they all said "Pockets!" Judy laughed. "Okay let me work on that and in the meantime, check out the selection I have here," and she disappeared behind a wall.

They got up and looked at all the dresses and began to try them on. They tried on short dresses, pant suits, and unnecessarily puffy dresses. They tried on black dresses, yellow dresses, and green dresses. But when Judy came back, she had a new color pallet of dresses with her. The navy blue and the wine color dresses caught the attention of everyone, including the bride, and they all had pockets.

By the end of the day, the girls and bride had settled on a plum, velvet, floor length, long-sleeve deep-V dress, with pockets.

Twenty

You Again

"Your mom is out of surgery and making her way to recovery now," the doctor said to Piper and Matthew. "After going in I did find more of a mass then we originally suspected, but I feel it all went well. You can go home and get some rest. You won't be able to see her tonight, but we will call you in the morning and let you know when she's up for visitors," he said. He continued to explain the recovery process and that even though they got most of the mass, they were unsure just yet if the tumor was cancerous or not. They were sending off the biopsy and would have more information soon. As of now, if she progressed in a positive way, she would be home in a few weeks. The doctor got up and left the room and the siblings sat back in their chairs and laughed. They laughed because they were so sick of crying. They got up and made their way to their mom's house. After arriving at the house, Matthew walked in with Piper to make sure she got in okay like a protective brother would. He hugged her goodbye and left.

Piper noticed how late it was when she got back to her mom's house but decided to text Grace anyway. A few minutes after she sent the text, her phone rang, it was Grace. "Grace, I am so sorry, did I wake you?" Piper said as she answered the phone.

"No, I was up actually, I was waiting for your call or text. I just wanted to make sure you were okay. How did everything go?" she asked.

"It went as well as could be expected. If everything goes well, she will be able to be home to recover soon," Piper explained as she began to brush and floss her teeth. "I'm not sure how long I will be here for. I sent Stephanie an update and told her I was not sure when I would be back, but I could work from home. The worst part, aside from the possibility my mother has cancer, is that I need to drive Dad's old truck around for a while. I hope it still runs," Piper trailed off.

"Okay, do you have a few for me to tell you something?" Grace asked.

"Yeah, of course, what's up?"

"It's very possible you were right about Daxton; you know being engaged or something," Grace said humbly.

"I'm sorry Grace, I didn't want to be right. How about we go out when I come back, you can fill me in, and we can get your mind off everything? But are you okay?"

"I don't know, since I'm not a hundred percent sure, I still have hope. We can talk when you get back. I will check on you tomorrow," she said.

"Well Grace, there is one more thing," Piper asked. "When did you hook up with Matthew?" Piper asked like a little kid. Silence took over the phone then Grace spoke.

"Okay so I will check on you tomorrow. Love you," and Grace was off the phone.

After disconnecting her call with Grace, Piper absorbed the information from her mom's doctor, and it settled into her brain, she could not help but think of her mom and feel so grateful that she was still here with her. They had a healthy relationship, but she still needed more time with her mother. She wanted her around to see her get married, hold her grandkids and to help through both the tough parts of life and the good times of life. She could not imagine not being able to tell her mom she was engaged, go wedding gown shopping, or have her help pick out a wedding venue. She knew she would need her mom for so much more before and after that. Exhausted, Piper crawled into bed and planned to see her mom in the morning.

The next morning Piper woke up to the sound of her phone ringing. Pulling herself out of a comfortable slumber, she grabbed her phone and saw her brother's name across the screen. Paranoid something was wrong, Piper jumped up and was quick to answer the call.

"What's wrong?" Piper asked into the phone.

"Nothing, I just wanted to see what time you would be at the hospital today?" Matthew asked.

With relief in her voice that her mom was okay, she let him know she would be getting ready to head to the hospital in about thirty minutes. She hung up and pulled her blanket over her head.

After showering, eating a slice of toast and putting her coffee in a travel mug, Piper pulled on a sweater over her T-shirt and made her way to her dad's old truck.

As she drove towards the hospital, Piper called to let Stephanie, her boss at TOGETHER, to let her know she was taking some time to stay in Ardentville and would be working from there indefinity and Stephanie gave her the okay to work remotely, but let Piper know she would still have to show up for events when necessary. When the call was ending, Piper began to smell smoke and her dad's old green Chevy began to buck.

"Great," Piper said under her breath and pulled the old truck over to the side of the dirt road she took to get to the hospital. Slamming the door behind her, Piper tied up her hair in a bun that sat on the top of her head and opened the hood to the old truck.

Not knowing exactly what was going on with it, she began to scan what she could see through the now building smoke. She remembered what her dad had taught her about the old truck and tried to see if she knew what was going on with it. Just as she was wiping the smoke away, she heard a honk. Looking up from under the hood, she could see what looked like a figure walking toward her. And then she heard a voice. A voice she could pick out of any crowded room. A voice that was both familiar and stomach turning at the same time.

"What seems to be the problem?" the voice asked concerned.

Piper inhaled deeply knowing exactly who was walking toward her and her mind suddenly presented memories she had banished to the back of her brain. Their first kiss under the tree in Parker's Park when they were in middle school. Him showing up at her house to pick her up for junior prom wearing a bright yellow tux that not only didn't match her pine green backless gown, but was not the agreed upon tux. Her memories fast forwarded to the first exchange of "I love you" and everything that happened before their final goodbye. As Piper looked up her eyes met with the familiar light blue eyes that belonged to Blake Powell.

"Piper," Blake said matter of factly, looking right at her as if he had just seen a ghost. The two, frozen in time, looked at each other for what seemed like hours but in reality, was mere seconds.

"What, what are you doing here?" he questioned as he stumbled on his words and did that behind the neck scratch he always did when he was nervous.

"Blake. Hey," she said shaking herself out of her shock that he was standing in front of her after all this time. "It's my mom," she began and Blake interrupted, "what? What happened? Is she Okay?" he asked with fear in his voice.

Blake has always had a good relationship with Lucy. Up until the breakup, which was so painful, he removed himself from not only every aspect of Pipers life, but from Ardentville altogether. After Piper left, so did Blake. He went to Africa for a few months to clear his head but fell in love with photography after he took it up as a hobby. Once he sold a few pictures of the wildlife to a few big-name magazines, his unintended career took off.

"She's okay, we think," she said with sadness in her eyes and her words. "She had brain surgery and she's in the hospital but should be home soon according to her doctors," she said.

"But why are you here?"she asked curiously.

Blake looked at her directly, almost as if all the pain and suffering he had endured when Piper chose her career over him came rushing back directly to his heart, and said, "well, Piper, I am glad your mom is going to be okay, but I am not in the mood to have a civilized conversation with you right here on the side of the road. Looks like you need a tow, I will call it in for you," he said with distain and began to walk away, leaving Piper on the side of the road.

"But, Blake," she called.

Blake stopped in his tracks on the dirt road and

with a chill not only in the air but also in his overall demeanor, he said, "what?" without turning around.

"You have a tow truck. Can you just help me?" she asked, knowing he was upset. But it made no sense for him to leave her there.

Piper watched as Blake got in the tow truck from his dad's garage and coughed a bit on the smoke his truck made as he tore off in anger or frustration. In the moment Piper could not tell how he was feeling. She climbed back in her dad's old truck, rubbed her hands together and for a few minutes, Piper thought about the last conversation she had with Blake.

After Piper told him about the job offer, he knew she would have to pick him or the job. He wasn't ready to let her go, but he had no interest in living in Boston. Too busy. Too loud. Too many people. Blake liked the pace of the small town. He liked knowing who his neighbors were, supporting small businesses, the carnival, the pumpkin patch, and the way Ardentville basically threw up Christmas turning the town into a winter wonderland. He was afraid if he left, in the way Piper wanted to, he would lose those feelings. He didn't want to "turn into a suit." He had a lot in Ardentville, including the mechanic shop he ran with his dad. He knew Piper felt differently. Selfishly he let her make the decision to leave. He was angry and wanted her to know it. He wanted her to suffer for leaving. He sat across from her and waited for her to announce she was taking the job, and when she did, he stood up from the table they were about to have dinner on, threw his napkin on the table, looked at her for 3 seconds and walked out. That was the last time they saw each other. A few days later Piper, feeling sick and heartbroken, packed up what little she wanted to take with her, put it in her car and left Ardentville, alone.

That afternoon after leaving her entire life as she knew it, and headed toward Boston, she cried. She cried so loud and so much her vision was blurred by the endless stream of tears falling from her eyes. She second guessed herself over and over. She grabbed the phone to call Blake, but then put it down. She was sick over the thought of losing him. When Piper got to the city, her apartment wasn't ready yet, so TOGETHER put her up in a hotel until it was ready. Sitting alone in her hotel room, Piper called and talked to Grace, who had been living in the city now for a few months. The two met up for a few drinks and Grace showed Piper a few of her favorite spots.

Minutes later the loud tow truck pulling up next to her brought her back to present day and she knew Blake called in to the garage for someone to help her.

Days later Piper found herself away from her mother and Ardentville and back in the city. Stephanie had called Piper to let her know she needed to attend an event over the weekend. Rand had left Ardentville and was back in the city and back to work. They had planned to meet up in the city if they had time, but their bond was becoming tighter since Rand was there for Piper during a dark time.

Piper arrived back at her apartment on Friday evening and planned to see Grace, Sydney, and Rachel that night. Since her event was Saturday night and she planned to be back at her mom's on Sunday, the only time she had to see her friends was Friday night. Since Piper was gone for a while, she was eager to see her friends again and get caught up with their lives.

Throughout the day Grace, Piper, Sydney, and Rachel engaged in a group text to make plans for the night. After a few discussions about where to go for dinner, drinks and maybe a nightclub, they decided on a Glam Girls' Night Out, each dressing as glamorous as they wanted. Piper made reservations for dinner at Club Louis, one of the city's newest hot spots with a month-long waiting list. Because of Piper's connections and the fact that she was still working closely with Louis, she had an in. And with a connection like Louis, the city was pretty much open for business wherever they wanted to go.

Grace left work early so she could go shopping to find something spectacular to wear. She knew Piper would have the best outfit for her to borrow, but she was in the mood to shop anyway. As Grace reached House Lyons, a high-end boutique, her eye was caught by a navy-blue plunge-neck wrap dress in the window that had hints of glitter throughout. As she walked in, she was greeted by a sales lady who, after a quick conversation, informed her that the dress was unavailable for immediate purchase, but one could be ordered and sent to her apartment in just a few days. As Grace looked around the store, she thought about the blue dress more and more. Although the dress would not be available for that night, she still wanted it. Walking out of the store with nothing but a receipt in hand and a smile on her face, Grace decided that for Glam Girls' Night Out, something in her closet would have to do.

Hours later Grace's apartment was abuzz with four women, laughing, talking, drinking, and plotting, but first they wanted to see how Rachel was doing with seeing Marcus again.

"It was a shock to see him honestly, and a total fluke he was at that party. But we sat outside, and we talked. I came clean with how I was feeling and then he told me his side of the story."

Marcus knew there was movement around him. He was aware of the cold fall night enveloping not only him and Rachel, but also the city that sat in the distance. His skin felt the warmth from the fire and his blood was feeling woozy from the wine he was sipping on. He saw Charles from the corner of his eye and behind him he could hear the low rumble of people enjoying their night. But his eyes. His eyes were laser-focused on Rachel. For the past hour or so he'd sat patiently listening to her tell her side of the demise of their relationship. As she spoke, he noticed her body movements, the shape of her mouth that was glossy in the reflective light of the fire, her long dark hair that wrapped around her neck and her eyes. The gray more present than he had ever seen before, or maybe he just never took the time to really look at the color and how it fit her so perfectly.

But it was her hands that caught most of his attention currently. He had always liked her hands. Tiny slender fingers that fit so perfectly in his hands while they were together or walking or watching a movie. The hands that he loved but would annoy him when they made their way to his body while he was working on a case. Hands that tried to hold him when he was sad or disappointed or even celebrating but he was too busy to notice and as she talked, he didn't realize how much he had taken her hands for granted. The way they were always trying to reach out to care for him. The way they felt when he finally let her touch him and get close to him. The way they soothed him and put him to sleep because he always felt so safe with her. And now looking at them, wondering if they reached out to care for Jared in the same way they reached out for him. He knew he missed her. He knew he messed up. But what he didn't know was if she was someone else's at this point.

He had never met anyone like Rachel before. The girls he dated before her, like Sloane, were beautiful and they seemed to like him. At first, they presented as if they were all in. As if they could love him and take care of him in the way he had always wanted. But after a few months, the masks would fall off. He called it the First Trimester Curse, because it took about 12 weeks for true colors to shine bright like a diamond.

As he got to know other girls, they seemed interested in him but then after a while their focus shifted from him to themselves. He realized that not a lot of women could hold conversations beyond reality TV and the latest celeb gossip. He had one too many Kardashian conversations and began to realize he could not take the majority of these women to an event without feeling as if they may embarrass him, so he didn't take anyone. He got to the point where a lot of his dating was superficial. Date nights downtown or drinking at a local bar, but nothing real, until he met Rachel. And things were great, until he took her for granted and didn't ever realize it was happening.

Marcus knew Rachel was not wrong for leaving. He knew he should have treated her better. He knew she loved him for him, and he knew if he got sick, hurt, or got bad news, Rachel would be there for him, no question. Marcus loved so much about Rachel, and he knew how she felt about him, he never thought she would leave. Until she did.

"I don't blame you, Rachel," Marcus began. "After you left, I was angry and hurt. A few days after you walked out of my place for that last time, I sat on my couch and opened social media to see what you were up to. At first, I thought you blocked me, so I had Oscar look for you. When he said he could not find you, I knew you deleted all of your social media. That made my ears perk up. I called you and the number was changed. Then I was worried. When your dad didn't take my call, I drove to his house. He invited me in and told me to just let you be. By then I was enraged. I blamed you. I called you selfish," he said as he looked off in the distance. He sipped his fresh wine, adjusted his legs and then continued.

"I honestly had no idea why you left, Rachel," he admitted, "I tried to find you. But with no luck, I had no choice but to move on. Or at least I thought I was moving on. I wasn't. What I began to do was place a Band-Aid over something that required surgery and then sutures." He looked at her, her eyes now focused on him and paying close attention to the words pouring out of his mouth. Marcus inhaled, rubbed his brow and as the fire illuminated his face and Rachel could see he had something more to say. Marcus felt it was time to come clean with Rachel.

"The first month after you left, I went out, a lot. I met with my friends; I drank more. I handed over cases to coworkers, and I neglected my laundry. I began to talk to other girls. I began dating, way too soon. I lied to those women, and I lead some on." Rachel's eyes opened, stomach dropped, and she took longer sips of her wine. "I was hurting so much, and I had no idea how to fix it. None. I thought if I got you out of my mind, I would begin to forget about you. I took everything you had given me, put it in boxes, and left it in a storage unit I leased specifically for those things. I began to take other women to my place," he admitted shamefully.

"But it never worked. No woman could make me forget about you." Rachel cringed and bit her bottom lip, trying not to say anything. She knew she was the one who left. From the moment she walked away what he did was none of her business, but it still stung. More than stung. "After dating, and sleeping around trying to numb the pain, I met someone," he said with a pang of guilt clearly present in his eyes.

"Oh," Rachel said while she swallowed her wine... hard. A silent pause sat between the two former lovers and suddenly the chill in the air had nothing to do with the fall night looming above them.

Twent-Two

Fire and Ice

Their plan was on schedule and in just a few minutes they would be heading down to the waiting Uber to whisk them to Club Louis. Just as Grace was putting on the final touches of her lipstick, she heard her phone buzz.

It was Daxton. "Hey babe. Sorry I was unable to call today. It's been so busy at work. I am having a guys' night out tonight, so I will call you tomorrow."

Grace rolled her eyes once again at her phone and took a step back so she could get a good look at herself in the mirror. For a second, she didn't recognize the person staring back at her. As she looked herself up and down, wearing a gold sequin mini dress with barely-there sleeves and a low-cut neckline, her blonde hair flowing past her shoulders, and her open-toed blush strappy heels, she smiled and realized she had no idea when the last time was that she dressed up like this. Boy did she feel good. Grace felt as good as she looked, if not better, and knew right then that Piper was right, she needed a night out like this. She put gloss over her lipstick, took one last look with a turn, and she was off for the night with her friends.

While at dinner, the girls drank and laughed. They

shared appetizers and conversation.

"So, Grace, where is Daxton tonight? Have you heard from him today?" Piper asked, sort of stirring the pot. Grace, throwing stabbing looks toward her lifelong friend, responded, "I did hear from him, he said he's having a guys' night out tonight."

"More like a bachelor party," Sydney said as she and the others laughed.

"Ha. Ha," Grace retorted, rolling her eyes. "I don't think he's engaged, but I do think he may be seeing someone else."

"What do you think it would take for you to see that he is just not worth it? That you deserve so much better?" Rachel questioned as her tone turned from playful to serious.

As Grace sat at the table with a drink in her hands, she scanned the faces of her friends. The friends that had been by her side for so much in her life, the good and the bad, and she was starting to feel as though they could be right. The ones who love her, truly love her would not send her down a wrong path. Maybe they were right.

"You know what, I think for tonight, we just have fun. Let's forget Daxton, and all the other guys leaving us confused, and enjoy this amazing place. We can sort him out tomorrow," Grace said as she raised her glass to the table of friends who were surrounding her with love.

Her friends smiled and all the women raised their glasses to meet Grace's glass and with a clink they all decided to enjoy their night without discussing Daxton.

After dinner, Louis ordered them a car to take them to Fire and Ice: a local rooftop bar that is "fire" in the summer as a tropical oasis and "ice" in the winter as an arctic blast. The girls were excited to go to a place they had never been before. Louis called ahead and got them a table outside on the roof in the winter wonderland.

When the girls arrived, they were taken by elevator to the rooftop bar. Walking through the doors they were immediately given warm furry jackets with giant hoods to keep warm, a hot drink, and hand warmers for the inside of their jackets. As they were guided to their table, they noticed a group celebrating a bachelorette. As they made their way past the group, one woman from the party cheered and welcomed them to the frozen tundra.

When Grace, Sydney, Piper and Rachel were at their table they sat down and took it all in. The seating area was designed to look like an igloo with an ice sculpture table that had ice shot glasses ready to pour shots of whatever was ordered. The seats looked like snowbanks, and if it weren't for the heating lamps around them, they would have been convinced they were sitting on actual snow. The DJ sat high on a snow-capped mountain and the other patrons on the dance floor were all wearing the same type of jacket, in different colors, to keep warm. Some were taking their jackets off while others kept them on. The music was loud and the bachelorette party at the table next to them was going nuts.

The girls' table came with bottle service, compliments of Louis. As Piper poured alcohol for her friends, they raised their glasses high. "To an amazing Glam Girls' Night Out. May we have tons of fun, tons of shots, and no boys!" Piper said over the loud music and their loud neighbors.

"Cheers!" the friends said in unison as they all drank their shots together. The night progressed, drinks flowed, and the group caught the attention of a few guys brave enough to approach them. The girls threw their previous "no boys" pact out, and eventually joined them on the dance floor. With their new friends who eventually included a few from the bachelorette party and a lot of dancing with even more laughter, Grace knew this girls' night was exactly what she had needed. An hour or so later as things started dying down, Grace excused herself to use the bathroom and heard a few girls walking in while she was in a stall.

"Isn't she going to be a beautiful bride?" Grace heard one faceless, bodiless girl say to someone else.

"She really is. Daxton is a lucky guy. I just hope he can stay faithful to her," another responded.

Grace, with her eyes now open wide, froze as she began to stand up. She instantly sat back down and began to listen with intent.

"Well, he is marrying her. I am sure he isn't the same guy he used to be. If so, Charlotte would not be saying 'I do' next weekend," the first voice commented.

The girls outside the stall washed their hands, dried them, and made small talk until eventually leaving the bathroom. Grace, still frozen in shock, had no idea what to do, and then her phone buzzed. With her mouth still open, she grabbed her phone that was in her clutch and opened it. It was a message from Daxton.

"Hey babe, feeling sort of wasted, can I come by? I am close. I miss you."

"Motherfucker," Grace said out loud. She stood up, washed her hands, and made her way back to the table. As she walked, she debated what to do. Should she approach Charlotte? Should she respond to Daxton and have him meet her there? Should she just leave it alone and walk away? She had no idea what to do.

As she got closer to the table, in her heartbreak and

her anger, she decided she would approach Charlotte. She would show her the pictures and the texts and tell her what her fiancé has been up to. She knew Rachel, Sydney, and Piper would have her back and she was ready. No woman should marry a cheater, Grace decided in her fury as she made her way back to the table. But as she got to the table, the bachelorette party had left. They were gone. Their table was nothing but a frozen ghost town covered in empty bottles, bright pink banners, and furry colorful jackets occupied by no one. Feeling defeated, she sat down, wrestled her jacket off while looking blankly at the table, and instantly Piper called for a car to take them home.

The Cake

They sat outside in late September on the balcony of their wedding venue and waited impatiently for the baker to bring out the flavors for their wedding cake. Taking in the view all around them of the changing leaves and the gray sky reminding them how cold the winters get in New England, they sipped wine and sat close. Silence sat between them, a silence that was familiar to a couple who were comfortable with each other.

"Hello to the happy couple," the baker said breaking the silence of the cool afternoon peace. "I am Rolando, and I have the honor of baking and creating your wedding cake."

They turned to each other and smiled.

"Hi Rolando, I'm—" Rolando cut her off. "I know who you are; you are the bride, and this handsome man is the groom,"

He smiled big and placed a tray in front of them, with waters nearby. He gave them each a utensil set with a fork, knife, and a napkin. He also placed a pad of paper and pen on the table.

"In front of you I have placed a tray of cake, frosting, and fillers. The first row is your cake selections. We have Red Velvet, a wedding favorite and classic. Next, we have carrot, German chocolate, caramel apple, and of course we have yellow cake." He looked at the couple who had smiles on their faces.

"The next row in the middle we have your fillers.

Raspberry," he pointed to the first one, "lemon, my personal favorite, strawberry, chocolate, apricot, and cream cheese," he paused. "Any questions so far?" he asked.

"None so far, we are just looking forward to eating all of this," the groom said eagerly.

"We are almost there sir. As for the bottom row," again, he pointed, "these are your frostings. We have buttercream, Chocolate ganache, Royal icing, and if you prefer your cake to be naked, we can accommodate that as well. So do you have any questions?" Rolando asked.

They looked at each other, both holding forks as if they were going onto battle.

"I have a question," the bride said.

"Yes, anything I can do," said Rolando.

"Do we get second servings?" she asked and they all laughed.

"I suggest taking a bite of cake, then filling and frosting and seeing how your taste buds respond. I have a pad and pen if you feel you may need to make notes. Now if I can't be of service, I'll be back soon to check on you," Rolando slowly backed up and turned to make his way through the doors.

"Are you ready?" she asked.

"I have been ready for this since the day we met." He tapped a bit of frosting on her nose, kissed her and they began their tasting.

As they made their way through all of the flavor combinations, they had their favorites, but at the end *of the day they decided on a naked, three-tier yellow cake with pink tiger lilies and white and pink roses flowing down the side. Baby's breath and baby roses sat between the bigger roses.*

"This will be a beautiful cake. Would you like to order a groom's cake?" Rolando asked.

"No, we have one on special order from a friend," she said as a big smile reached across her face.

Folding Laundry

The next morning was a rough one for the friends because of the previous night and discovering that Daxton was truly engaged. They sat around the circular table they had sat at so many times before at The Usual. Grace, who looked the worst—heavy eyes, messy hair, and no energy, was able to rally to meet her friends but didn't plan on staying long.

"How is your mom, Piper?" Rachel asked trying to break the silence and unsure of what to say about the Daxton engagement thing.

"I'll be heading back tomorrow to keep an eye on her for a bit," Piper paused and looked around the table.

"Grace, are you okay?" Sydney asked what everyone else wanted to know.

"No. Not really. Last night, when I got home, I put a search of their names in my computer, and their engagement website popped up," Grace said blankly. "I didn't open it. I'm not ready," she said as she put her head on the table. "Can we talk about someone else for a bit?" she asked.

"Sydney, how's Andrew?" Rachel asked, changing the subject.

"He's been traveling a lot but starting to move into

his new place. He has big ten-day trip coming up to London soon. But since The Lemon Bar cocktail idea is in full motion, it looks like it's going to happen soon."

"No way! Congrats! What's in London?" Piper asked as she munched on a muffin.

"He's restaurant touring. Checking out kitchens and talking to the pastry chefs," Sydney said noticing even her friends were thinking of him as just her boyfriend and not Andrew Casper.

"And you saw Blake?" Rachel asked. "How was that?"

"Annoying," Piper said, and she told them about the issues she had with her dad's old truck and how they led to seeing Blake again.

"Tell us more about Marcus, Rachel," Piper said with wide eyes. Grace lifted her head and Sydney turned to face Rachel in her chair.

"After I left, he told me he started seeing someone. Lolli," Rachel paused to notice the look on her friends faces.

"Lolli?" Grace said, "is she twelve?" The group laughed, and Rachel began to tell them what Marcus had told her.

"Hey!" The voice coming from behind Marcus yelled as he stood with a drink in his hand, his fourth of the night so far. Oscar, who was standing next to him, saw where the voice was coming from and alerted Marcus to the woman trying to get his attention. "I saw you walking in," she shouted as she tried to drown out the loud music the DJ was playing.

Marcus turned around to see a woman standing behind him, trying to talk to him. From his intoxicated blurry eyes, he could make out that she was blonde, shorter than he was and had basic brown eyes.

"Can I buy you a drink?" she asked as she noticed he had his hand to his ears motioning he could not hear her. As she pointed to her glass and pretended to take a sip, Marcus put it together and he grabbed her hand and lead her to the bar. Once closer together and standing at the bar, Marcus had a better look at her. His first thought was that she would do for tonight. But as he stood next to her, looking in her eyes, he was less than impressed. His thoughts instantly went to Rachel's unusual gray eyes. The way they lit up a room, glowed a little more when she laughed and how they looked at him from across the room when they were out together. Marcus shook Rachel out of his memory, slammed his hand on the bar and ordered a few rounds of shots for the three of them. Drinking the shots down and trying to get Rachel out of his mind he heard a voice and noticed the blonde girl he was with was trying to talk to him.

"I'm Lolli!" she shouted, again competing with the music, as she took another shot. "Hi Lolli. Let's go dance," Marcus said, unenthused, while putting his shot glass down as they headed to the center of the dance floor. Turning back, he saw Oscar shaking his head and pointing at his watch. Oscar placed his glass down and headed toward the door.

The next morning Marcus woke to a familiar sound coming from the kitchen. With his bedroom right off the living room and the kitchen close by, he could hear dishes clinking together and water running. He smelled coffee. He opened one eye slowly, and then he sat up straight. "Rachel!" He said out loud as he pulled the covers off himself and jumped out of bed. "She's back!" he announced to no one and slid on the nearest T-shirt he could find, and pulling on his shorts, he raced to the kitchen. Standing there in front of his sink, was not Rachel like he had expected. His heart, pounding with excitement moments ago, fell through his stomach as memories from last night came rushing back.

"Good morning sleepy head," Lolli said cheerfully, "I made you coffee, washed your dishes, and cleaned off your counter," she said as she walked closer to him handing him a mug that Rachel had given him for Valentine's Day years ago. "Your kitchen was a mess. I hope you don't mind I cleaned up a bit for you." She moved between the living room and kitchen as if she had been there before. Marcus, holding a mug he swore he had put in storage, was stunned. He remembered meeting her the previous night, drinking with her, and taking her home. The only time he was able to be intimate with someone was when he had Rachel completely off of his mind, and that only happened when he was drunk. But usually, he sent them off in a car or they left on their own. None of them had ever stayed over. He could not remember much of what had happened but looking at her now, he recognized her basic brown eyes. And it's not that Lolli was unattractive, she was beautiful. Petite in shape, blonde hair and a great smile, all things Marcus was attracted to, but she was not Rachel.

During his relationship with Rachel, he certainly found other women attractive, but not in the same way he was attracted to Rachel. He was attracted to not only her looks, but also her intelligence. She was always learning and growing. She had these weird bits of information she loved to share with him, but he found unnecessary. When she talked about them, her little nuggets, she called them, her face lit up.

But he was also attracted to the way she loved him.

He was attracted to how well she took care of him without him asking her to or even expecting her to. She did it because she wanted to. Even if other women hit on Marcus, he paid no attention to them because his heart, body, and mind all belonged to Rachel. But he didn't realize any of this until she was gone.

Now, standing in his living room, with a mug full of black coffee, he missed her even more and just wanted Lolli to leave, but she was talking, and cleaning, and his place had not been cleaned in a while and he could not find the energy to call a service. So, he added cream and sugar to his coffee and sat on the couch and began to sip. "She has to leave at some point" he thought to himself as Lolli talked on and on about her job or whatever it was, she was saying.

Over the next few months or so, as Marcus avoided healing after Rachel left, he continued to see Lolli on and off. But one night when he brought her out to have drinks with his friends, they had enough of seeing him miserable. The look on Oscar's face said it all when he saw Lolli was with Marcus. As they all sat around the table, everyone made small talk. They had met Lolli before but not enough to actually know her, but they knew Marcus was not interested in an actual relationship with Lolli in the way she looked to be interested in one. She got up and excused herself to go to the bathroom and Oscar took the opportunity to say what the others were thinking.

"It's clear you are not interested in her; you are not over Rachel. What is going on?" Oscar demanded to know.

Marcus sat still and looked away from Oscar and got up from the table. "Can we talk outside?" Marcus asked Oscar and the two made their way outside just as

Lolli was walking back to the table.

Now standing outside under a bright streetlight, Marcus put his hands in his pockets and told Oscar about the pain he was still in. How much it hurt to wake up every day and that work was falling apart. He went on to tell him he thought Lolli was nice but could not stand to look at her face when she is sitting where Rachel used to be.

"I fucked up man. I fucked up big time. She left. She left, didn't say goodbye and I have no idea how to find her," he paused, inhaled, and then continued, "I had no idea how good she was for me. She was genuine and she was natural. I did not think she would leave. I thought she was being dramatic and needy. But she wasn't. I was selfish and I have no idea why I am like this. I put my career above her always. I never rotated my priorities. Yes, my career is important, but she was too, and I neglected to see that when she was right in front of me," he covered his face with his hands, rubbed his face and then sat down on the curb,

Oscar sat next to his friend and placed his hand on Marcus's shoulder. "I know. I know how hard it has been since Rachel left. I can see it; we can all see it and we are worried about you. It's been months. She's not coming back. It's time to heal and move on," Oscar said, still sitting close to his friend. A voice from behind them got their attention and they got up and went back inside.

Later that night, Marcus laid in bed. He had a heavy, but sober mind and he thought about the conversation he had with Oscar. He was thinking maybe he was right and maybe it was time to move on from Rachel. He wondered if he could have something more with Lolli. He realized he was not giving her a fair chance and maybe he should, maybe he should take the time to get to know her and see if there was possibility of letting Rachel go and moving on with Lolli.

The next morning, Marcus woke up thinking he would feel better, but he still had Rachel on his mind. He knew he needed to decide. He had to either really try to make it work with Lolli or let her go. When he thought of letting her go, he wasn't sad. But he also knew she was good to him. So why not just try it? Why not put in a little effort and see how it goes? He needed to get his life back on track and he knew he needed to make this decision in order to help him do that. Work was suffering, he was drinking too much, and he had a heavy mind about losing Rachel in that way. Knowing she was not coming back, he still had to figure out why he took her for granted in the way he did because he did not want to make a mistake like that again.

That night after work, Marcus invited Lolli over. Marcus decided to see if he could see anything with her. He thought she was attractive, she took care of chores around the house and never asked for anything from him, but he wanted to see if she could carry a conversation. See if she would embarrass him at a work event. He wanted to see who she really was. Maybe he could not see she was actually amazing and more than just basic brown eyes with blonde hair. Maybe she was intellectual and maybe she could add value to his life, but he was too focused on his broken heart to see it. He decided to let all of that go and really put in effort to see if maybe she was more than what meets the eye.

"At work today," Marcus began as he poured himself some wine, "I looked at taking a course on leadership. Since I have been thinking about joining a private firm, I have to prepare for more responsibilities, and I'm interested in leading more," he said as he sat down on the opposite side of the couch from her. "I was reading up on the importance of vision in the work-."

Lolli interrupted, "yeah I agree with that," as she sipped her wine while looking at Marcus.

"Agree with what?" he asked confused.

"You should have your eyes checked at least once a year. You know, to have good vision. It's important," she stated as she smiled, feeling confident.

Marcus stared at her and questioned whether he should explain, but instead he agreed with her and took a large gulp of his wine. As the two sat on opposite sides of the couch, the dryer buzzed, and Marcus got up to fold the laundry. Folding laundry was not something he would choose to do, but he needed a few minutes to himself to go over what had just happened in that conversation.

As he stood in front of the dryer folding his clothes, he wondered why Lolli just didn't get what he was saying. With his face scrunched up and piling up his clean shorts one on top of the next, he could not imagine how a kindergarten teacher was so clueless. Just as he pulled out one of his shirts, he noticed something hanging from his favorite red T-shirt. He turned on the light and placed his shirt on the dryer and his mouth instantly dried up as he pulled a ball of black hair from the shirt. He thought back to getting irritated with Rachel because her hair was always all over the place.

"'One day when I'm gone, you will miss my hair.' she'd say and laugh. "She was right," Marcus whispered while looking at the hair and grabbing it in his hand. He closed his eyes for a split second and strongly exhaled. He turned around and seeing the back of Lolli's head on his couch where Rachel used to be saddened him and in that moment, he knew what he had to do.

"That's a lot to take in Rach," Sydney said.

"What are you going to do?" Piper asked. "Do you think you may want to try again?"

"I'm not sure. I need some time, but I will admit, I'm glad we are talking again," Rachel said.

"I hate to do this, but I have to get going to get ready for my event," Piper said.

A few hours later, after she had said goodbye to her friends, hugging them tightly because she had no idea when she would see them again, she got ready to head to her event that was planned for later that night. Piper had to get to the grand opening of Chandelier. TOGETHER was hosting an event there for all of the previous swipers who found their matches on the TO-GETHER app.

Chandelier was the perfect place to host such an event. Chandelier, formally an old warehouse that was deemed condemned, was turned into a new modern nightclub/exclusive event. The décor being mostly glass and light pinks, also boasted refurbished luxury chandeliers from all over the world. The ceilings were high, and the chandeliers hung low. The dance floor looked as if it was covered in diamonds. Piper made her way around the building, inspecting every aspect of the beautiful facility, while Stephanie, Piper's boss, made her way around with a guided tour by Franco, the main investor in Chandelier.

When Stephanie and Franco had drinks one night, they came up with this idea of bringing all of the successful connections made by either the TOGETHER app or the match-making service, and Stephanie knew Piper would do this event justice. The only catch for

192 | KELLY SMITH

the ones attending with their matches was that each person had to bring someone single to the event. Piper was over-the-moon excited to have been asked to oversee this event.

Hours later, after making sure the caterer was all set, the cake was on display, and the staff and owners of Chandelier well informed about the night's events, Piper headed back to her place to get ready. Sporting a bright-red, floor-length open-back gown covered in rhinestones and wearing nude platform heels, Piper made her appearance and walked the red carpet from her car to the front door of the Chandelier. With cameras flashing and music coming from inside, Piper felt both like a movie star and proud of herself for the way the event was turning out so far.

During the night everything went off without a hitch. Laughter and chatter could be heard from all over. Music played and people danced, and new connections were made. By the end of the night, Piper was exhausted and decided to head home. As she got into her car and took her shoes off, she heard her phone buzz. Looking down she saw the name and a smile flashed across her exhausted face. Rand's text was letting her know he had made brunch reservations. She responded and the two sent messages back and forth a few times and then Piper put her phone down and went home.

That night Piper unzipped her dress and left it where it fell. She stepped out of it, washed her face, brushed her teeth and then in a fresh pair of pajamas, she crawled into bed and closed her eyes. For the first time in a while, Piper felt good. Happy.

The next morning waking up, Piper felt refreshed and was excited to see Rand. She popped out of bed, made her way to the kitchen, and had some coffee, while she called to check on her mom. After a quick conversation with her mom, and her mom letting her know she had to see the doctor soon for a checkup, and letting her know she would be heading back to her house in a few hours, Piper got up to get her day started. As she took a shower and washed her hair, Piper was feeling excited to see Rand again. She made her way out of the shower, dried herself off with a towel, wrapped another around her head, and made her way to her closet to find outfit. With the weather colder than usual, she opted to go with jeans and a sweater. Nothing fancy, but also nothing too casual. With her navy-blue chunky turtleneck and tighter-than-usual jeans on, she dried her hair and put on her makeup. Just as she was finishing getting ready, a text came in.

"I am excited to see you today." It was Rand. Piper held the phone in her hands and with excitement filling both her heart and head she responded, "me too."

After responding to Rand, Piper gathered her things to head back to Ardentville after brunch. She loaded her suitcases in her and felt relief that she no longer had to drive her dad's old truck. She knew once she got back to Ardentville, she had to pick up the truck and see Blake. Although she asked her brother to pick it up for her, he said since Chase had not been feeling well, it wasn't much of a priority. She slammed her trunk shut and made her way to see Rand.

Hours later, after brunch ended and Piper was on the road, she had time to go over a lot of things in her head. She thought about her mom, who was now home and feeling better. Although it was a Sunday, Piper took a call from Stephanie and explained to her that her mom had just gotten home from the hospital and would need care for at least a few more weeks until she would be okay on her own again. Stephanie let Piper know she didn't have to be back into the office until after the holidays since Piper was doing great managing to work from home and attending work events.

After the conversation with Stephanie, Piper felt happy to be able to be with her mom through the holidays. At brunch with Rand today, she'd learned that although he mostly practices in Boston, he does work in Ardentville a few days a week so they could see each other if they wanted to even with Piper not being in the city full time for now. With the way things went at brunch, Piper for sure wanted to see Rand again, and soon.

Going To The Chapel

A few days had passed since Grace discovered Daxton was indeed engaged. A few days since Grace discovered that what she had with Daxton was nothing but a lie. A few days since Grace put Daxton and Charlotte in a search bar on her computer and found their engagement website full of pictures of their relationship, friends, family and from when they were kids. A few days since Grace discovered the happy couple is to be wed in a few days. That is when Grace began to search for alcohol.

She called in sick to work, ate nothing but peanut M&Ms, and drank all the alcohol she had in her apartment. Rachel and Sydney stopped by but Grace was not ready to talk yet. Now, as Grace got up from the couch dressed in her robe, headed toward the kitchen to open another bag of candy, she heard a knock at the door. Frozen in fear for a second, she thought of who it may be on the other side. Daxton had been reaching out, but she never responded. Although his last text was one saying he would be away for work for a few days and would call her when he came back. So she knew it wasn't going to be him. According to the time on the microwave in the kitchen, her friends should be at work. Grace slowly walked to the door trying not to make any noise and looked through the peephole.

"Cory? Friggin' Piper," she whispered to herself.

"Yes Grace, it's me. I heard you, so open the door please," he said, determined.

"I can't, I'm busy. I.. I.. I have company. I will talk to you later," trying to convince him to leave.

"I have Salisbury's," he held the bag in front of the peephole knowing that would convince her to open the door.

"Damn it," she said as she unlocked the door, letting Cory in.

"Hey," Cory greeted her with a frown as he put the box of pizza and bag of subs on the counter in the kitchen.

"Hi," she responded in annoyance. Hunger swelled in her stomach with the smell of food he brought over.

"Come here, give me a hug," he said walking toward her.

"No, no I stink. I can't hug you. I can't do anything," she moved away from him.

Cory grabbed Grace and pulled her in tight and close. As he hugged her, she tried to resist, but moments later she hugged him back and began to cry as he held her. He let her cry for a few minutes, then led her to the couch. As she sat down, he went to the kitchen and made her a plate of food. He brought it to her and then made one for himself. They sat on the couch mostly in silence, looking out of the window over the city's gray cold evening. The sun was setting, and the city lights were beginning to glow, and suddenly, snow started falling.

"Do you want to talk about it?" Cory asked as he grabbed both now empty plates and walked toward the kitchen.

Grace looked at him with big sad eyes and felt guilty and mad and upset with herself, but she was also glad Cory showed up. She looked at him, and said, "yes."

As the former couple sat on the couch in Grace's living room, they talked about everything. From their own relationship to how they go to the place they were now both in. Grace single and hurt, and Cory still just single.

"I'm sorry you are hurting right now Grace. Honestly, it's difficult to see your pain and I'm not sure if that's because you are truly hurt, or because you are hurt over another man," Cory said with his heart open and on his sleeve. Grace looked up at him, confused. "When we broke up, I couldn't function. I couldn't move. I was so destroyed. It seemed to have come out of nowhere, and it paralyzed me for months. I couldn't go out, or to work. My friends tried to get me out of the house, but I wouldn't budge. I didn't shave, shower, or eat very much. It was all I could do not to call you. Then, a few weeks before I saw you, I began to feel better. I got up and shaved. I got moving again. The day I saw you, with him, I was on my way to meet a girl I had been set up on a blind date with," Cory looked away, pained. "When I saw you, my heart lit up. But then he was there, and he dragged you away from me. And you were gone. Again." Cory picked up his drink to soothe his dry mouth. "I thought about going after you," he said after he took a sip, "and I even started walking in the direction you left in. But then I figured you were where you wanted to be. So, I let you go, and I went home."

"That day I saw you, my heart lit up too," Grace said with tears in her eyes. Now looking directly at him, she said, "part of me wanted to run to you, grab onto you, and leave with you." Now looking down shamefully, Grace continued, "at the time I thought I wanted more. I thought I wanted what you couldn't give me. I thought Daxton wanted to marry me. But he didn't." Grace felt a sickness in her stomach knowing she let Cory go for no good reason and now he was sitting next to her on the couch taking care of a heart he didn't break. "I'm sorry Cory. I really am. I messed up and made an awful mistake by letting you go." She poured out her heartfelt words, hoping maybe this could be fixed.

"I miss you, Grace. Every day," Cory said as he reached out his hand and gently placed it on Grace's leg.

She slid her hand over his and squeezed tight. "I miss you too Cory."

"Would you like to go out with me Grace? We can take some time and talk over dinner and drinks?" Cory asked as if he was talking to his school yard crush.

"I would actually love that, Cory," Grace said through a smile she had not had on her face in days.

After they got a little more settled into the night, and after Cory convinced Grace to take a shower, Grace opened up about Daxton and a plan she had formulated, and Cory said he would support her 100% and help in any way if she needed him to.

"Can you take me somewhere on Saturday if I decide to go?" she asked him.

"Should I ask where or just agree to take you?" he asked with a raised eyebrow.

"Just agree," she said as a smile began to appear on her face.

Grace woke up to a gray, snow-filled sky. With the annoying buzzing of her alarm echoing in the background from her night's sleep, she reached over her white down comforter and shut off the noise maker that ruined her peaceful slumber. As she rolled over to look out the window from her 18th floor apartment, she could see the peaks of the city covered in a blanket of snow. She hugged her pillow tight under her forearms and exhaled as deeply as she could. She stared out the window and tried to study each snowflake as it fell. She found herself lost in thought and wondered how she was going to handle her plans for the day. She closed her eyes, inhaled, exhaled, and then opened them again.

Without moving her exhausted body too much, and still holding her pillow under her arms tightly, she turned to see her navy blue, low cut, tight around the hips, make-you-look-better-than-you-actually-do, dress that House Lyons had delivered days before, hanging outside of her closet door. Reluctantly, she rolled over and got out of bed, grabbing the dress on her way out of the room and headed to her usual first thought of the day, coffee. She walked to her kitchen to make her special "wake me up and give me mental stability" concoction.

As her magic potion began to brew and the scent of French vanilla filled the air around her, she looked down at her cell phone that had been charging in the kitchen all night and saw a few missed texts and a voice message. The voice message, she knew even before looking at the name, was from Daxton. Her stomach dropped when her thoughts were confirmed; his name laying squarely across her screen. She didn't know if she should listen to the message or not.

She allowed herself to be still while sipping her coffee. She let minutes pass and ideas fill her head. She knew if she was going to do what she had planned, she had to leave her apartment by 10 a.m. Right then she made up her mind; she was going, and nothing was going to stop her. She texted Cory asking him to pick her up at 10 and his response was so quick, she thought maybe he was waiting for her text. He was. Cory was hoping to see her that day, and every day after.

Grace got up, jumped in the shower, and got ready. By 10 a.m. there was a knock at the door and minutes later, with Grace dressed in her House Lyons' tight, navy blue, low cut, glitter-all-over dress, they were headed to the church.

Grace stood alone in the doorway of St Peter's Church, not too far from her apartment. As she looked down the looming aisle, she inhaled. Moments later when asked by a young usher, "Bride or Groom?" She boldly said, "groom." She was then led to a row close to the altar. She took the closest available seat to the aisle. An older lady sat on her right, and the usher led in a family of five who sat to her left. She sat watching the church fill up with excited guests while avoiding small talk because the knot in her stomach would not allow her to speak. About 20 minutes later she heard the door in the front of the church open and men dressed in black tuxedos spilled in. They were loud, laughing, and full of chatter.

As Daxton took his position at the altar, his friends hugged him and patted him on the shoulder. His face was covered in a smile, and he looked genuinely happy. Soon after he took his place, the organ began to play and one by one each bridesmaid made her way down the aisle.

One at a time Grace could place their faces from the previous weekend. As time got closer to the bride making her way to marry Grace's current boyfriend,

Grace thought about leaving. She questioned what she was doing. She had no business there. Just as she decided to go, the entire church stood up and the wedding march began playing.

The church doors opened and there stood Charlotte, her dark brown hair that had hung low with curls past her shoulders on the night of her bachelorette party now twisted up and behind her head. Her green eyes gleamed and Grace could see tears beginning to swell in them. As she stood in the doorway of the church, her white wedding gown fit her slim figure perfectly. In front of her she held colorful flowers with one hand and with the other held the hand of a man who was probably her dad. She was a beautiful bride.

Grace's heart broke in her chest and then sank to her stomach. She hated that Charlotte had no idea who Daxton really was. Grace didn't look at Charlotte much longer before turning her attention towards the groom. Grace looked at Daxton and within an instant, Daxton's eyes met Grace's. From where Grace was sitting, she could see the color drain from his face. His eyes were wide, glued to her and not his bride. Grace watched as his friend nudged him a bit before shifting his eyes back towards Charlotte.

Once the bride reached the altar and as the priest carried on with the vows, he looked around the church and announced, "if anyone knows any reason these two should not be joined in holy matrimony, speak now or forever hold your peace."

Grace waited a few seconds while everyone looked around, some laughing because no one ever speaks up at that point in a ceremony. When Grace felt enough time had passed and all eyes would be on her, she stood up. When she stood, just as she wanted, all eyes were on her, including the groom's.

Whispers infiltrated the church. Grace made eye contact with Daxton for one second, closed her eyes and stood there. She counted to five, and then slowly but deliberately made her way back down the long church aisle with her head held high, her shoulders back, making sure she made eye contact with no one. When she got to the doors, she opened them and walked outside to Cory who was leaning against his already running car at the bottom of the church stairs for her. As Grace walked calmly down each step, her smile grew. She was satisfied with the way she handled herself in the church and with Cory waiting for her with open arms, she knew it was okay to begin again.

"Feel better?" Cory asked with a big smile, opening the car door for her.

"Absolutely," she responded with a smile on her face, and as Cory held the door open for her, she kissed him on the lips and got in.

Twenty-Five

Decisions, Decisions

Rachel sat home days after accidently running into Marcus at the book reading. She sat in her apartment at dusk, took in the city and thought back to their conversation.

Rachel sipped her wine and held back tears as he told her about getting into therapy the day after he found the hair on his shirt. How he broke it off, whatever it was, with Lolli and knew he had to heal from losing Rachel. With the night growing older and the air seeming colder, the conversation between the two continued to flow. Marcus told her about therapy. The tough days and the long nights of unpacking his baggage from his past with ex-girlfriends and how his childhood played a big role in how successful he wanted to be. How he had a difficult time with balance. And how he had to accept himself for who he was and work on things as they came.

"I stopped dating," he said boldly. "I had to heal so much of what was broken in me before I could invite someone new into my life. I worked on my career and on myself. I hung out with my friends and didn't drink for a while. I was able to get back into the gym and I started to volunteer at the animal shelter. I was seeing things through a different lens," he said as he looked right into her gray eyes and felt a warmness run through him. "A healthy lens," he finished.

"Wow Marcus. That's incredible. I'm proud of you," Rachel leaned in closer to him and poured more of the wine Charles left for them on his second round of checking on the fire. In mere seconds so many thoughts went rushing through her mind. She could see he was no longer the person she had left 12 months ago, and frankly neither was she.

The love she had for him never went away. She felt that in order to be with him or with anyone, she had to be whole first and know whoever she was with could be there for her in the same way she would be there for someone else. Swallowing hard and nerves jumping off of her skin, she spoke.

"It sounds like you have done a lot of healing and soul searching over the past year. Your new job sounds incredible, and I love that you volunteer with animals. What do you think is next for you?" she asked hesitantly with her stomach in knots.

"Well Rachel, I think showing up here with one of my coworkers who happens to be the cousin of the author is a sign. I think we were destined to meet tonight. Closure or maybe something more. Seeing you again has been amazing. I have not stopped loving you," he said.

Rachel melted into his words, and she grabbed his hand and squeezed three times.

As Rachel was getting up to make dinner, her phone rang. Grabbing her phone, she saw it was Marcus.

"Hello?' Rachel answered the phone.

"Hey Rach. How are you?" he asked.

"I'm okay. How are you?"

"Can I come by? I want to talk to you. I want to see you."

"Do you think that's a good idea right now?"

"Yes. I think it is. I let you walk away from me once and I was miserable. You leaving taught me how much I love you and I want to spend time with you again. I'm not asking for a relationship; all I am asking for is time, Rachel," Marcus pleaded.

Rachel was still for a few minutes, wondering if she could trust him not to make her feel disposable again. The pain she had felt for so long never left her and it scared her. But what if he has changed? Was he worth the risk of heartbreak again?

Twenty-Six

Yes or No

One afternoon, just after Sydney got home from the meeting officially turning The Lemon Bar into a night venue as well as a bakery, her phone rang. Looking at the screen, she saw it was Andrew. He had been in London for the past 10 days touring restaurants, hotels, and resorts giving lessons and training to the staff and was not due back for a few more days. When she saw it was him, she picked up instantly, slightly concerned.

"Andrew?" she asked, "everything okay?" With the time difference she didn't expect to hear from him.

"Hey Syd. Yes. I'm okay. I was calling to let you know I will be arriving back in the city tomorrow and I want you to pick me up from the airport," he said.

"Okay. Why are you coming home early? Is your driver not available to pick you up?" she asked, "But yes of course I can pick you up."

"We have a few things to talk about when I get home. I have something to tell you. And it can't wait," he said, making her stomach drop, "I'll send you my flight information, but I have to go. I love you, Sydney," and before she could say anything, he was off the phone.

The next day Sydney drove nervously to the airport. She had no idea what was going on with Andrew. She kept hearing his cold voice in her head. The way he spoke to her and then how he was just gone. She had fears of what he had to tell her. What if he cheated on her? What if he was breaking up with her? As she drove, she turned on her radio to see if maybe music could drown out her overthinking. But it didn't work so she called Piper.

"What do you think he wants to tell me?" she asked.

"Maybe he wants to ask you to move in with him but he's nervous?" Piper said.

"Could be that or maybe he has a secret baby," Sydney said and gasped.

"I don't know Syd, I guess you can just wait and see what he says. You are just torturing yourself and honestly, we are not helping right now," Piper said.

Sydney hung up with Piper after hearing updates about her mom's progress. Piper wished her luck and assured her that no matter what she would there for her. Sydney parked her car, gathered her things and the bottle of water she brought for Andrew and made her way into the airport.

When she walked through the doors, she found her way to the arrivals station, checked to see if his flight was on time–it was–and she took a seat until she saw passengers funneling down the escalator. Sydney stood up and positioned herself in front of the escalator to be sure she could see him as he made his way down to her. After a few minutes she looked up and saw Andrew. He was standing at the top of the escalator, signing what looked like autographs. She stood there and watched him smile, shake hands and pose for a few pictures.

He looked happy, and the happier he looked, the warmer her body felt. Her body was filling with warmth because that is how love felt as it made its way through her veins. She was excited, calm, safe, and terrified all at the same time. Although she had no idea what Andrew needed to tell her, she did know she loved that man, and she didn't want to lose him. As a tear or two began to race down her cheek, she saw Andrew get on the escalator. As she looked at him, he spotted her. And from where she was standing, she saw his smile and then his teeth. He waved a small gentle wave at her, and she felt her body warming again.

As he made his way toward her, she felt giddy. She moved toward him through the small crowd, and Andrew dropped his bag and embraced her. He grabbed her by the waist, pulled her in close and hugged her tight. He pulled away slightly and kissed her on the lips. She could feel his excitement. Pulling away and laughing, she handed him his water and he grabbed his bag and then her hand. As they stood waiting for his luggage, he marveled at her. Smiled and squeezed her hand.

"You are beautiful Syd. I missed you so much. I am so happy just standing next to you right now," he said, slightly emotional. Sydney looked at him and could not help but wonder what he wanted to tell her.

"I missed you too Andrew," she said, trying to muster a "how was your trip," but couldn't. She just stood close to him and held his hand.

About an hour later Sydney sat across from Andrew and she had all the answers she didn't have that morning and was in shock. She felt as if she had no bones, no muscle. She sat across from the man she loved and felt as if she were a bag of skin.

"Sydney. Say something. Anything," Andrew pleaded.

"What am I supposed to say to you Andrew? What exactly am I supposed to say to this? You made a decision. A huge decision that will impact my life and you didn't talk to me about it first," she said with hurt and anger beginning to grow inside her.

"This was a decision for me. Not a decision for you. I didn't need to talk to you before I made it. This is my life. This is my career. I am the only one in charge of my life. Not you." Andrew spit out in a harsh tone and instantly regretted it.

Sydney sat in shock and the tears were piling in, but she refused to let him see her cry. She got up, looked at him straight in the eyes and said, "Andrew, I love you, but this is over. I will not stand in your way." She grabbed her bag and began to make her way out of his place. As she got to the elevator door, she opened it, looked back at him, and got on the elevator and just like that, she was gone.

Sydney cried the entire way home. When she got home, she called Piper, who then called the others, and within 30 minutes Grace and Rachel were rallied around Sydney with wine and Chinese food. Piper was headed back to the city for a night or two for an event and she would join them when she got back.

"Wait," Grace said, "he got his dream job at a restaurant in London, and he's moving there in a few weeks?" Grace asked.

"Yes," Sydney said as her tears poured out and she could hardly breathe. "And he didn't ask me what I wanted. What about me? How could he not consider me in this? Do I not mean anything to him? Did I ever mean anything to him?" She cried out.

"Syd. I know you are upset, and I can see why, but he's Andrew Casper. You had to know he was going to eventually get a job like this, he's talked about it," Grace said, trying to be both supportive and realistic.

"I know," Sydney said still through tears, "but what about me?" She cried.

"We know," Rachel said as she hugged her friend, "but you have to let him live his life. Maybe you could go visit?" Rachel added.

Sydney sat on her couch, slightly intoxicated, and felt sad. Heartbroken. The man she loved was leaving. She has lost another man she loved.

"Hello?" Piper said into her phone seeing it was Andrew.

"Hey Piper, it's Andrew," he said sadly, "I think I messed up."

"Yeah, I would say so. I'm headed back to the city right now. What's going on?" Piper asked.

Andrew sat at home with the lights off and as he made his way onto the balcony looking at the city below him as he told Piper about his job offer and how upset Sydney was with him. He explained he didn't want to lose her, but he had worked so hard throughout his life to get this exact job. He didn't want to choose between the woman he wanted to spend his life with and the job he wanted to do for the rest of his life. Did he have to choose? Did he make the wrong decision, taking this job without considering her? He asked her. After talking to Piper for a while, he got up and ended the phone call. He knew exactly what to do and he was going to do it with no regrets.

The next evening, Sydney got a call from Piper asking her to meet her out. At first Sydney hesitated and resisted. But Piper insisted it would be good for her to just get out. To stretch her legs. Sydney thought that was a weird thing to say, but Piper had never led her down a wrong path, so she agreed to meet her out.

Sydney got up and took a shower. Well, the shower took her. Sydney stood under the hot shower and didn't move. When she felt like she had enough, she dried off and put on jeans and a T-shirt. As she began to put her makeup on, she lost interest and left her face with just mascara. Sydney checked her phone for the 500th time in hopes she would hear from Andrew, but nothing. As she dragged herself out of her apartment, her phone rang. Sydney jumped at the sound and looked at her phone.

"Grace," she said to herself, "hey Grace," she said unenthused as she answered the phone, "what's up?"

"So, change of plans for tonight, we are meeting at Redwoods," Grace said.

"Redwoods?" Sydney said as she looked at her outfit. "Why?" she asked.

"Not sure, Piper called and said Louis got us in," Grace said simply.

"Well fine. But I'm not changing," Sydney said. And she headed to her car.

Once at the restaurant, she saw Piper and Sydney and regretted not changing her clothes.

"What are you wearing?" Piper asked standing in her silver heels and wearing a tight red cocktail dress.

"You are lucky I am out of the house and not crying," Sydney said as she hugged her friend.

"Okay let's go to the table, everyone is already here. We are just waiting on you," Piper said as she grabbed Sydney's hand and led her to the elevator to take them to the rooftop deck where they had a table waiting for them.

As the elevator doors opened and Sydney and Piper walked out, Piper let go of Sydney's hand and stepped to the left joining her other friends. Sydney looked at Piper, Grace and Rachel all dressed up and looked down at what she was wearing. "What am I missing here?" she thought to herself.

As Sydney turned around, she saw the patio covered in twinkle lights, a violinist in the corner quietly playing and a pathway of candles. Sydney looked at her friends who were mouthing to her to follow the path. As Sydney followed the path she looked up and she saw Andrew dressed in a suit holding red roses, and she could see tears filling his eyes. Sydney looked back and saw her friends leaving. They blew her kisses and waved goodbye to her. She turned to face Andrew who was now down on one knee…

The Flowers

"*Are you happy?*" *he asked through a smile on his face. "I have no idea what a bridal bouquet should look like, but what you picked out is beautiful.*"

"*Yeah,*" *she returned his smile, "you know I love lilies. Remember when you sent me flowers that first time and you had no idea they were my favorite and each time you sent flowers again you just sent the same bouquets over and over?*" *She looked at him with love in her eyes.*

"*I remember I took a lucky guess,*" *he said as he laughed, "and if you say you like something I will just do that thing over and over. But I had no idea I sent the same ones?*" *he said with a surprised look on his face. "Why didn't you say something?*"

"*Like what? Hey, stop sending me the same flowers? No way. I loved those flowers whether they were the same or not, they were from you,*" *she leaned in for him to kiss her and he did.*

"*Okay you two, I have your order here. Let's go over it before you leave,*" *Sylvia said as she pulled out two chairs near the greenhouse.*

"*For the bride,*" *she smiled at the bride, "we have a beautiful 10-inch bridal bouquet with white tiger lilies, plum roses, and navy callas. The bridesmaids will each carry an 8-inch bouquet with plum and red roses. And for the gentlemen they will each wear a plum rose boutonniere. We will have the flowers for the tables at the wedding venue and I have a 4-inch replica of the bridal bouquet for you to throw to all the single ladies." She paused and looked at the couple, "does that sound about right?"*

"Sounds great," she said while they both began to stand up.

"Okay, we are all set then for February 12th. I am so happy for you guys. And thank you for sharing your story, it's absolutely beautiful and I'm grateful to be a part of your happy ending. You went through a lot to get here. This is what true love is."

Saying Goodbye

Pulling into her mom's driveway in her own car felt familiar to Piper. She parked her car, shut the engine off and gathered her bags to head inside. As she shut the trunk of her car with both hands full, she could see her mom standing at the door waiting for her. Seeing her mom standing in the doorway, Piper felt relief and sadness. She was happy her mom was finally home from the hospital, but she was sad she was not there when Matthew brought her home. With a smile on her face and happiness in her heart, Piper made her way inside.

After unpacking her things into her childhood bedroom, Piper made her way to the living room where her mom was resting on the couch. They sat together for a while and talked and laughed. Piper made dinner and poured wine for herself. She helped her mom to eat and then helped her bathe and put on her pajamas. Although her mom felt helpless, she let Piper help her. After giving Lucy her meds, they snuggled close together on the couch close to the roaring fire Piper built for them. As her mom began to doze off to the holiday rom com playing on the TV, Piper's phone buzzed.

216 | KELLY SMITH

Blake: I hear you are home with your mom again. How is she?

Piper: she is resting and feeling okay. Thanks for checking in.

Blake: Glad to hear it. Are you picking up the truck soon?

Piper: I can come by tomorrow to get it.

Blake: I can swing by and pick you up on my way in, so you don't need to find a ride?

Piper: Okay. Not too early though

Blake: 10?

Piper: That works. Thanks.

With that last response, Piper closed her text screen and laid her head near her mom and listened to her mom breathing. As Piper closed her eyes, her phone buzzed again. This time it was Rand. Piper shot up and quickly opened the text.

Rand: How are you? How is your mom?

Piper: Hi. I am doing well. The ride back was good. And my mom is sleeping on the couch next to me. We were watching a movie and she passed out on me.

Rand: I am glad the ride went well, and you are back safe. One on one time is good. Sorry to have interrupted.

Piper: You didn't interrupt. I am glad you texted.

Rand: Good. I am too. I have been thinking about you.

After a few more minutes of texting, Lucy woke up and Piper helped her to bed. And Piper made a bold decision to video chat with Rand.

The next morning Piper found herself sitting uncomfortably next to Blake in his truck on her way to pick up her dad's truck. Fortunately, the ride was a quick one, but it was full of odd small talk. As they drove, Piper could not help but notice Blake. His beard growing in thicker than she remembered. His hair was cut perfectly, as always. His hands, although a bit older, still looked strong as they hugged the steering wheel. As he drove and she took all of him in, his scent that swirled inside the truck, she wondered if she still had feelings for him, buried deep inside or if she had been able to fully let him go.

When they got to the garage, Blake walked Piper inside the small waiting room and went to get the truck. Making his way through the glass doors, Piper watched him take his coat off, revealing his still very much in-shape body. The way his black long-sleeve thermal shirt hugged his body made his muscles and hard work in the gym evident. She heard him talking and laughing. That laugh was something she had no idea she missed until it flooded her ears. She took a seat with a heavy heart and tried to understand how she was feeling. Moments later Blake made his way through the doors and called for Piper to go with him, and she did.

Making their way to the back of the garage, Piper could see her dad's truck and as they walked Blake filled her in on what was wrong with it.

"Nothing major was wrong with it, the carby needed to be replaced, that's all," he said without making eye contact.

"Carby?" Piper questioned.

"Oh yeah that is how they say it in Australia, I learned that when I was there. At times I like to spice things up," he said, laughing.

"Okay, so the carby needed to be replaced," Piper said without enthusiasm.

"Yes," Blake said as he stopped laughing and cleared his throat.

As they stood in front of the truck, Blake opened the driver's side door and then hopped in to start it up. Piper stood close by and watched as Blake turned the key and the truck started up. A smile creeped on Piper's face at the sound of the engine. Blake sat in the driver's seat and took in her smile and his heart sank. Suddenly without warning, he cut the engine and hopped out of the truck. With all the emotion he had been holding in for years he looked at Piper and said, "do you regret any of it? Was it all worth it?" he asked with a mixture of sadness and anger strong in his voice.

"What?" Piper said, defensive.

"You know what. Do you regret at all moving away and leaving me? Everything we had. Everything we worked for. The plans we made to be together. The house on the corner of Maple and Rosewood, the one we drove by every Sunday and imagined our kids playing in the yard. Do you regret it?" he asked with passion, making direct eye contact with her.

Piper, stunned and caught a little off-guard, reached in and dug out the emotions and feelings she had been pushing down for years. All of those "I don't want to talk about it" moments came crashing through.

"Do I regret making a decision to build a career and make something out of myself? No! I don't and I never will! I worked hard to get where I am, and I could not have accomplished what I have in this small town. I did what I needed to do in order to be who I am, and I will never regret that," she yelled, feeling as if she had to defend herself.

"Why? Why, Piper? Why did you leave me? Why was it so easy? Why were you able to go and never look back? I loved you. I wanted my life to be with you and you left. You left me!" Blake shouted in anger.

"You were the one who could not possibly leave this town you love so much," she yelled as her arms motioned to encircle the town. "You are the one who looked me dead in the eyes and said you would not leave Ardentville to move to Boston and then, weeks after I left, took off halfway around the world. How do you think that made me feel? You refused to support my career a few hours away but left everything you said you loved to get over me in another country. Why, Blake? Why was I not enough for you to move a few hours away?" She shouted now, tears running down her face.

"You didn't want me. I could not live in a place where everything reminded me of you, of us. I was hurting and I had no idea what to do. The one person I always had to rely on was gone and wanted nothing to do with me. I had never felt so empty in my life. I wasn't eating. Sleeping. I felt as if my body was crawling with bugs, and I wanted to peel my skin off. I was going mad. I was lost and I needed to feel better, so I left. I went to the airport for what I thought would be a few weeks away but when I got to Africa, I felt better. I was warm again. The bugs I felt on my skin were gone. I was breathing and then I was eating. Leaving and staying gone was never my intention. It just happened. All of this just happened. I never intended to go to Africa. It was the only next available flight, so I mindlessly got on that plane. I had no idea it was taking me to my new life," he said, now visibly exhausted. He was releasing years of toxic feelings and sadness. Anger and hurt. Frustration and rejection. Emotions were running high.

Piper's heart was racing from adrenalin and the tears kept coming. Blake sat down on the floor of the garage, put his face in his hands, and cried. Piper let him cry for a minute, then made her way to him. She sat next to him and put her head on his shoulder and grabbed his hand. Blake threw his head back and looked at Piper. With red eyes and a stuffy nose Blake smiled at her. "I have not cried since you left. I have been holding it in. I was so broken, but now I feel whole again. It took a while but I am. I know things happen for a reason and today after all of that heartbreak and confusion I have this amazing career that I am in love with. And now sitting here looking at you, I have the closure I didn't know I needed. I feel relief. But I miss you," he said, drying his eyes.

She leaned into him and felt the same way. For the next few hours, they sat on that floor in the garage and talked and laughed. Within those hours pieces of them that were broken began to repair themselves. When Piper's phone buzzed, she saw it was Rand. She looked up at Blake and then down at her phone again.

"Piper?" Blake said, "do you think we could try this again?" he asked. "Do you think we have both grown enough and now that we are both older and have lived more life that we could end up in that house on the corner of Maple and Rosewood?"

"I don't know, Blake," she said as she stood up. "I have to go. How much do I owe you for the truck?" she asked blankly not expecting him to ask her that.

"No worries. It's on the house," Blake said as he got up and handed her the keys.

Piper drove back to her mom's house with a heavy heart and a heavy mind. She took in all that Blake had said, realizing she had no idea how much pain he was in. All this time she had convinced herself that he was just selfish, and she held onto that anger for so long.

Now, with reality staring her in the face, she was even more confused as to how she felt than she had ever been.

When her phone buzzed it woke her from her trance. Matthew was asking her to pick up the dessert he had ordered from Carol's Bakery and Pastry Shop. Piper had almost forgotten they made those plans while she was in the city. Taking a sharp left, Piper headed to Carol's to get the cherry cake. She was relieved to see her family to take her mind off of the morning's events with Blake, but she knew she had to unpack all of it soon, especially since Rand texted her to let her know he was going to be in town that following Tuesday. He wanted to take her to dinner.

Over the next few weeks, the relationship between Piper and Rand had blossomed. They texted and video chatted when they were apart and began to spend more and more time together when Rand was in town. One evening as Rand was leaving the office, he invited Piper over to have dinner and possibly watch a movie.

Piper was met at the door by Rand. With a big smile across his face, a tight black V-neck T-shirt hugging his chest and jeans that fit his body just right, he welcomed her in. Piper walked into a homemade meal waiting for her. At first, she was convinced he had ordered it and was trying to play it off as if he made it, but after seeing the dirty pots and pans in the sink she quickly realized he had made the dinner himself.

The music coming out of the surround sound was peaceful and light. The smells of roasted chicken and rosemary filled the room and as Rand lit the candles, Piper noticed the roaring fire. Handing her a glass of red wine, Rand removed his apron and the two clinked glasses. They sat in the warm cozy living room and chatted while they drank their wine before sitting down to dinner. Rand asked Piper about her day and the two talked about work and how Lucy was doing. After eating and enjoying dinner together, Rand led Piper back to the living room and sipped on more wine.

"Meeting you, Piper, was such a surprise," Rand said as he scooted closer to Piper. "I was so fearful of dating again. I had no idea if I would ever want to attempt it, but this, it sort of just happened. I have no idea what may or may not come of this, but I am willing to find out," he said as he took a sip of his wine.

"I feel the same way Rand. I guess I felt a connection to you right away. You have an ease about you," she said sincerely as thoughts of Blake and his words reappeared in her mind. Taking another long sip of wine, she convinced herself she could distract herself and stay in the moment with Rand.

Just as Piper finished her wine, Rand leaned in and kissed her. Piper, placing her glass down, leaned in and kissed him back. Forgetting all about Blake, Piper was all in on Rand and what she hoped was about to happen.

She had wanted to be intimate with him since the first date, but she was not very aggressive. But tonight, with her body full of wine, she could, in a way, be someone else, someone more aggressive. She was attracted to Rand, his looks, his mind, his character. Rand was an overall good man. He was respectful of her, listened to her when she had both good and bad days and paid a lot of attention to her. With Rand, she felt as if she could really be herself and he simply accepted her for who she was, flaws and all. And she accepted him. She was comfortable and she was ready to show him how she felt about him, and she did.

Kissing on the couch led to touching on the couch

and then clothes coming off on the couch. Piper, now on top of a half-naked Rand, looked into his eyes and her body felt warm. Rand, beginning to sit up, lifted Piper off of him and led her to his bedroom. In his room illuminated only by a few candles, Rand began to peel off the rest of Piper's clothes.

Slowly and deliberately, he made his way down until he had nothing on. Taking her toned, naked body in, Rand began kissing her. Starting with her neck and made his way down to her legs and then back up again. While his lips explored her, his hands did too. He wanted to get to know each and every inch of her body. He wanted to know what turned her on and what didn't. That night he found out. She laid on her back, feeling him all over her body. She rocked back and forth, and she enjoyed his touches. Her body had chills one minute and overheated the next. She felt the power of his hands. The more he explored, the hotter the room felt. The entire night was all about Rand getting to know Piper's body and Piper getting to know his.

That night Piper slept at Rand's house, close to him. He held her and the two had pillow talk until the early morning hours, eventually both falling asleep in each other's arms. Waking the next day, Piper felt fresh and happy. She woke to the smell of coffee calling her to get up. Walking into the kitchen she saw Rand finishing up the dishes and when he noticed her, he got her a mug and filled it for her. He grabbed a mug for himself and sat next to her on the couch. As the comfortable silence of early morning surrounded them, it began to snow. It was the first snowfall of the early winter season. Piper laid her head on Rand's shoulder and Rand gently kissed her forehead. As the quiet moments passed, Piper felt full.

224 | KELLY SMITH

On her way back to her mom's house Piper replayed the events of last night and how she felt about it. She thought about Blake and what he had said the last time they spoke. The last thing she wanted to do was get more involved with Rand if she still had feelings for Blake. Not only would that be unfair to her, but more importantly it would be unfair to Rand, and she could not do that to him.

As she pulled into her mother's driveway, she picked up her phone and sent a text to Blake asking him to meet her. She figured seeing him again and having a conversation with him may help her to clear up how she was actually feeling about him. She needed to know if he was truly the one who got away or if it was really over and she could move forward with Rand with a clear conscious. Almost seconds after sending Blake a text, he responded and said he would be willing to meet up. Before walking into her mom's house ready to face a bunch of questions, she had agreed on a day, time and place to meet Blake.

Walking through the front door of her mom's house, Piper spotted her mom resting on the recliner watching a movie.

"Hi Piper. You just missed Matthew, they came by for a few hours and brought by their new puppy, Sadie. Such a cutie. How are you?" her mom asked, seeming like she was in good spirits. Piper held her breath, waiting for her mom to start asking questions about her whereabouts last night.

"Oh no. A new puppy huh? Now I am sorry I missed them," Piper said as she laughed.

"Yeah. Total cutie. Go put your stuff away and come sit with me for a bit. I missed you last night," she said and pulled up the blanket to her neck. "Oh, and can you bring me some Ibuprofen? My head hurts a little," she asked.

"What? Your head hurts? What's wrong? Did something happen?" Piper asked anxiously.

"No, no nothing happened. I think it's a run-of-the-mill headache. Nothing to worry about," she said calmy.

Piper picked up her phone and texted Rand, asking if it was okay to give her mother something for her headache and if so, how much. He responded instantly and said she could have some Ibuprofen and told her what to give her. He also strongly suggested she make an appointment as soon as possible to get it looked it. Piper gave her mom what Rand told her to give her and then went to shower. After showering and feeling better, Piper made her way to talk to her mom in the living room.

"So, Piper. Tell me what's going on. Tell me about Rand, and I want to hear how things ended with Blake when you picked up your dad's truck," she stated.

"How did you know about Blake?" she questioned before realizing they live in a town where everyone knows everything.

Lucy gave her a look, and Piper was more than happy to spill the beans and tell her mom everything. It felt good to get all of it out. The frustration. Confusion. The feelings she had for Rand. She told her mom what Blake said and she went on to tell her about last night with Rand.

When Piper was finished and exhausted from replaying all of it, her mom looked at her and said, "Every time you say Rand's name, your face lights up unlike anything I have ever seen," she said with a knowing smile on her face. Piper looked at her mom and could not help but smile and her face began to turn red.

"It's okay to move on, Piper. What you and Blake had was amazing and you learned a lot. But you both left. Regardless of why, you both left. Is it a beautiful romantic notion that after years of living apart you come back together and live happily ever after? Yes, it's a beautiful idea, but Piper, do you want to live in an idea or in something real? I would hate for you to lose out on someone as amazing as Rand just so you can have a romantic notion with someone who didn't or could support your career. With someone who was unable to show up for you when you needed them to. As much as I love Blake, and I really do, you needed Blake to fight for your relationship years ago, not now, not today. Not after you have made something of yourself. What you could have with Rand would be beautiful. It won't be a walk in the park, but Rand is the type of man you build with. A man who won't leave. A man who seems ready to accept what you have to offer. I think the way you are thinking about Blake is how you remember him years ago. My best advice to you Piper, and then I will let you decide, is to never trust a man who walked out on you when you needed him the most," she said with as much sincerity as she could. "Now I am going to go lay down. I feel tired," she said as she slowly got up.

"I think we should make an appointment to see the doctor. Just to get things looked at," Piper said, worried.

"I think I will be okay, but if you think we should, then let's do that," her mom agreed as she made her way to her bedroom.

Piper sat alone in the living room of the house she grew up in. Looking around, taking it all in, she was happy to be home, but memories once again of her and Blake infiltrated her mind. She took in everything her mom had said but she had no idea how to figure out how she truly felt. When thinking about Rand, she felt it on the inside. She felt warm and happy. Rand was starting to look like he was a good for her.

But when she thought of Blake, all she really had was memories of him. She had no idea who he was today, and if she even wanted to find out. She was meeting him the next evening and she would be open-minded and try to see how she felt near him again. Piper got up and began to make dinner for her and her mom. As she cooked and set the table, she got a text from Rand. Piper's blood rushed with excitement.

Rand: Hi. I just got back to the city. How's your mom?

Piper: Hey there. Glad you had a safe drive. She is resting. I am going to make an appointment for her tomorrow.

Rand: I will call Betty in the morning and make sure she is seen first thing. I am glad she is resting. Sorry I am not there for a few more days.

Piper: Thank you Rand. It means a lot to me. I am sure she will be okay with Dr. Baker. But I wish you were here.

Rand: Me too.

Piper made her way around the kitchen as she prepared dinner and texted Rand. Just as she was setting the table, she heard the doorbell ring. She let Rand know someone was at the door and she would text him after dinner. Opening the door, Piper was shocked to see Blake.

"Blake?" Piper said, confused.

Blake made his way in before being invited and

kissed Piper, hard. Piper began to push him away but then feeling something familiar, something comforting, she let him kiss her and she kissed him back. Without a word exchanged between them, the two fell back into each other as if no time had passed at all. Her mom resting in the other room, Piper and Blake made their way to Piper's room as hands groped and clothes were taken off. Ending up on her bed, they wasted no time. It was quiet and quick, but intentional. After, with Blake still laying on top of her, Piper panicked when she realized what she had just done. Although she and Rand were only dating, nothing official, she felt guilty and felt happy at the same time. She was confused. Wordlessly, the two got up, cleaned up, and got dressed. Piper needed to be alone and to give her mom dinner and she walked Blake out. At the door he grabbed the handle, turned and kissed Piper on the mouth.

When he was safely on the other side of the door, Piper sat at the table with her head in her hands. Utterly confused now, more than ever, Piper got up and went to check on her mom. She was terrified her mother had heard them. She was afraid of walking into her mom's room and seeing her sitting the bed with those "I know what you just did" eyes.

Walking into her mom's room and feeling slight relief that she was still sleeping, Piper called her name to wake her up for dinner. She called her name a few times and when her mom didn't respond, Piper turned the light on and saw her mom looked pale and was not responsive. Piper grabbed her cell phone and called 9-1-1.

As the ambulance arrived, Piper had already called Matthew and he was standing by her side. The EMTs were able to rouse her but took her to the hospital. Piper and Matthew followed the ambulance in his car. At the hospital Matthew and Piper sat next to their mom in the emergency room. Lucy was awake and alert but exhausted and her headache was not getting any better. Feeling relief that they were in the hospital, Piper could breathe just a bit. The emergency room doctor came in and told them they were going to run some tests, scans and some blood work. While they did that, they were going to call her neurosurgeon to inform him of what was going on and let him know the results of the tests.

Hours later and after a bag or two of fluids, Dr. Baker came in and let them know that Lucy was dehydrated and that caused both her headache and her exhaustion. Although they knew what it was, they wanted to keep her overnight for observation. With it being close to 11 p.m., the siblings said goodbye to their mom and got into Matthew's car on a cold dark night. The two made small talk and Piper told Matthew she had been thinking about moving permanently to Ardentville.

"Piper. No. I will not let you do this. You have worked too hard to get out of here just to leave an amazing career to be here again. I am here. You are a few hours away. You have to live your life," Matthew said and then paused. "Does this have anything to do with seeing Blake again?" he asked. Piper turned her head to look at him.

"No. It has nothing to do with Blake. I am worried about Mom. I don't want her to live alone. What if I wasn't there tonight? Yeah, it was dehydration, but what if it wasn't?" she said, holding back tears.

"I know. But she's going be okay. I just don't want you to relive your teenage years with a guy who might have been your husband. I want you to be truly happy. Look," Matthew said pulling into his mother's driveway, "do you remember Faith? From high school?" He asked Piper as he put the car in park and turned to her.

"Yeah, you thought you were going to be with her forever," Piper answered.

"Yeah, well did you know that weeks before my wedding, she reached out to me and I saw her?" he asked. Before Piper could answer, Matthew continued, "I saw her, and I was almost convinced that I was making a mistake. That I didn't want to marry Laura, but that I wanted to be with Faith. And then I realized Faith was in my past for a reason. That didn't contribute to making me the man I am today. Faith was great, but she was just a steppingstone to the life I live now. You have no idea how grateful I am every day that I didn't listen to nostalgia and even more grateful I didn't do something stupid before I got married. I think, at times, exes will come back into our lives to shine a light on the amazing person we currently have in our lives. I don't know Rand very well, but I like how he makes you smile. Blake was great, but his time is over." Matthew said as he stared off into the dark night.

"Wow. Matthew, I had no idea," she said as she reached over and hugged her brother. As he hugged her back, he began to cry.

"I needed this hug because I am worried about Mom too and I needed to have this conversation with you," he admitted. Once inside, Piper and Matthew agreed to go to the hospital in the morning. Just as Matthew left, Piper's phone rang. Noticing it was Rand, she pressed decline and took a shower instead. As she dried off, put on pajamas, and crawled into bed, she got a text from Rand.

Rand: I wanted to check on you. Here if you need me.

Piper reached over, shut off her light and with a heavy heart and mind, went to sleep.

Weeks later Matthew and Piper sat near their mother laying in the bed, nonresponsive and colorless. The siblings knew the end was near. While in the hospital with dehydration, Lucy caught pneumonia. The doctors tried everything they could, but the infection was too strong for Lucy's already weakened immune system. Piper informed Stephanie of her mother's condition, and Stephanie gave Piper as much time off as she needed. Piper had asked Grace to come to Ardentville and she was arriving that afternoon to be with her.

Over the last weeks, between the guilt she was feeling over sleeping with Blake and her mom being sick, Piper was not talking to Rand very much. She missed him every day and although he tried to visit her while he was at the hospital, Piper never agreed. She had not spoken to or heard from Blake since that night. She actually heard he left town again to take a job in England. When she realized he had left, she was hurt, but not surprised. Now she had bigger issues to worry about. Not only was her mom dying, but Piper was throwing up and had no appetite. Not sure if it was from stress and missing Rand, or if it was something more, like an illness, Piper pushed it down and tried to focus on her mother.

While in her mother's hospital room, waiting for Grace, Piper got up to get some water. In the hallway as she made her way to the water fountain, she saw Rand and he saw her. Standing in the hallway with her eyes set on him, she suddenly felt weak. He made his way towards her and as he got closer, she reached out her arms to him and he grabbed her. As he held her, Piper cried and collapsed. Rand picked her up and brought her to a closed empty room and laid her on the bed. Sitting next to her, he held her hand and let her cry it all out. He got up and got on the bed with her and held her until she stopped crying. He wrapped his arms around her tight and squeezed her so she knew he was close and how much he cared about her. Piper cried about how sorry she was for not talking to him and how much she missed him. She told him how hard things were and that everyday all she wanted to do was see him. As she talked, he listened. And then suddenly, alarms went off. Piper sat up as she heard people running in the hallway, Rand let her go and he got up with her. They were running towards Lucy's room.

Days later Piper, Matthew, Laura, Sydney, Andrew, Grace, Cory, Rand and Rachel stood in the cemetery on a cold winter day, surrounded by many of Lucy's friends, extended family, neighbors and much of the community. Piper began to speak.

With the sun out and shining bright, Piper stood in front of so many who loved her mom. In a dark dress, a long overcoat and a red scarf Lucy gave Piper years ago, Piper eulogized her mother.

"Today is a day that is always coming. With each day that passes we are closer to death. Although this is a fact, we never acknowledge it until we have to. I never thought about this day. The day where I would stand in front of so many to talk about my mother, our mother, in the past tense. I could stand here and tell you I am sad for the loss we share today. I could stand here and tell you I have no idea how my life will go on without her.

"But today, I want to talk about her. Her memory. The life she lived both before and after she had kids. Our dad loved our mom. He loved her out loud, even on the days when she probably didn't deserve it. The best gift a dad can give his kids is loving their mom, and he gave us that gift each day."

"After our dad passed, our mother was never the same. She was still kind and giving and funny. She showed up for us and for the people she loved, but something inside her changed. Over time, we got used to our dad being gone, and pieces of her were showing up again, but she was never the same."

"As a mother, she was fierce. Protective and a disciplinarian. We got away with nothing on my mom's watch. And I think that is why Matthew and I have turned out the way we did. I am grateful for the life I have because my mom formed me not only as a human but as a woman. She is the woman I hope to become when I grow up. So, Mom, I want to tell you I love you and I will miss you every day. Thank you for being strong and for being weak. Thank you for showing me I can make mistakes and then I can fix them. Thank you for tough love and for the embraces of reassurance when I was scared. Thank you for opening my eyes when they were closed so tightly. I will think of you on during the first snow fall of the year, during the fireworks on July Fourth, and when I become a mother for the first time. You, Mom, are loved."

Piper placed flowers on her mom's casket and walked over to stand next to Rand, who grabbed her hand and squeezed it three times. The preacher said a few words, and Matthew decided not to. After the ceremony was over, and hugs were given out, Piper pulled Grace aside to talk to her.

"How are you feeling Piper? You okay?" Grace asked while she hugged her friend. "You did a great job talking about your mom. She would have been so proud of you," Grace continued.

234 | KELLY SMITH

"Thank you, Grace. It has not been easy. I miss her so much. But listen," Piper said, "I need to tell you something."

Grace looked at Piper with concern.

"I'm pregnant," Piper said.

Two Years Later

❧

Together

Marcus and Rachel
Request Your Presence
At Their Wedding Celebration
Friday, February 12th
Five o'clock in the Evening

River Valley Winery
Reception to Follow

"We made it," Rachel said excitedly to Marcus as they packed their car to head to the wedding venue. Marcus leaned over and kissed Rachel on the top of her head before shutting the trunk of their car.

"I know. It was as long road, but I could not be happier about how it all turned out. I can't believe I get to marry you in a few days," he said to her with light in his eyes. "Let's agree now that we are a team. We stick together and no matter what, we don't freak out. As long as at the end of this weekend I can officially call you my wife, that is all that matters." He grabbed her hand; kissed it and she agreed. "My wife." His smile is from ear to ear. He shook his head in disbelief and smiled more at her. She smiled back and got in the car, and he shut the door behind her.

The drive will take a few hours and on the way to River Valley Winery, they both answered calls, made a few calls and practiced their first kiss whenever the opportunity presented itself. Along the way they check flights for delays and make sure each room at the venue is set up for the babies and kids that will be arriving with her friends.

"It looks like Syd's flight is on time from Heathrow. I hope she feels okay while traveling. She's only four months along but I am sure on that flight it may not be comfortable. But oh, I can't wait to see little Andrew Junior! I bet he is so big now," Rachel squeals with excitement as she looked at her phone reading texts.

"I am quite sure she will be well taken care of on Andrew's private jet. It is amazing how well his TV network took off. And The Lemon Bar, who knew Syd had such great business sense?" Marcus said. "And I'm sure it's easier to travel with a small child on a private jet too," he continued. "What about Grace and Cory, will they be here on time for the rehearsal dinner tomorrow night?" Marcus asked. "I know they were just getting back from their delayed honeymoon."

"Yes," Rachel said, "they land tonight and will drive in the morning to the venue. I am so excited to see them. I can't believe it took them so long to get married. I know it was a rough go after all the that happened with Daxton," Rachel said while rolling her eyes. "I can see why Cory wanted to wait a bit before popping the question."

"Oh yeah. I missed all of that drama. Man, I would have loved to have seen Grace show up at that church. No surprises from you this weekend, I hope," Marcus said with great laughter, grabbing Rachel's leg.

"Not from me, Marcus, I hope you don't have any surprises for me. I know your little friend Lolli had a hard time letting you go," Rachel said in a snarky jealous tone. Marcus cleared his throat and tried to change the subject.

"Well, what ever happened with Daxton? Did he ever get married?" Marcus asked.

"He didn't. In a twist, I guess another girl had said something to Charlotte the night before the wedding and she didn't want to believe it. You know, that's hard because they had planned their wedding and it is exciting, but if you get mystery people popping up at your wedding and he cheated before, it is best to cut and run," Rachel said. "He tried to reach out and get back together with Grace, which is why Cory was slow to get engaged. But after seeing a therapist and working through a few things, they were able to build again. Thank goodness," Rachel's phone rang and stopped her thought process. "It's Piper!" Rachel said quickly answered the call.

"Piper, how are you? You okay?" Rachel asked.

"Hi, are you a full-on blushing bride right now? You have your handsome man next to you?" She asked in a teasing way. Rachel's face turned red, and she looked at Marcus who already had smile on his face looking at her.

"Now I am, Piper. And yes, we are headed to the venue now. You okay? How's it going with Tessie? Is she still a spitting image of her dad?" Rachel asked.

"She is great and of course she is. She's also a bit cranky because she misses her daddy, and I am cranky because I miss her daddy too," Piper explained.

"Oh no. Is Rand still away for his conference? Will he be back soon?" She asked.

"His flight landed about an hour ago so he will be here soon. I can't wait to see him. I know it was just a few days, but I love that man and I miss him when he's gone," she admitted. "We will be leaving here in the morning to head to the venue. Do you have a plan for everyone to meet or are we just getting together for the rehearsal dinner? And what about Syd? Any idea when her fancy jet arrives?" Piper asked.

"No plan as of yet. I know we have to meet up with the family etcetera tonight. I hope to see you guys before the rehearsal. I was actually just telling Marcus that Syd's flight looks like it will be on time. And Marcus seems to think all is well on the jet as far as comfort goes. I can't wait to see her belly," Rachel said.

"It has been so long since we have all been together. When was the last time? Cory and Grace's wedding? Oh, Rand just got home, I have to go love on my husband. I love you, you beautiful bride, and I will see you both tomorrow." And with that she was gone.

As they got closer to their wedding venue and closer to the rest of their lives together as husband and wife, Marcus reached over and grabbed Rachel's hand.

"Are you happy, Babe?" he asked.

With a smile on her face and his hand safely in hers, she looked over at him and said, "I have never been happier. I love you and I can't wait to be your wife. Thank you for loving me."

The End

22244105R00141